My Sister's Keeper

Dalyn Woods

In A Race Against Time

Naval Commander Nathan Harper will pay any ransom for his sister, Emma. But the kidnapper's demand is more than he bargained for – a secret formula linked to Megan Foster, the woman who destroyed his family.

Megan carries the guilt for Emma's abduction, and so much more. She's determined to find her, even though it means enduring Nate's contempt.

Together they battle the clock, nature, and shadowy enemies. When forced to choose, will Nate protect his heart or surrender to the woman who threatens to invade it?

Acknowledgements

Who knew that through the heartbreak of Alzheimer's dementia, I would find healing in writing?

During the past six years of caring for my mother, I have had the opportunity to pursue a dream. The stories swirling around in my head were finally able to be poured onto paper and now, unbelievably, published.

Although much of writing takes place in solitude, this is not a solitary effort. Many people have spoken a word of encouragement at the perfect time to keep me in the pursuit.

Angela Vigil took a chance on the amateur in a room full of professionals. Heather Webb and Susan Kicklighter graciously polished me. In doing so, these three women made the dream seem possible.

Lorraine Haataia introduced me to the value of a critique group, which is now my weekly addiction.

Linda Wood Rondeau turned me from business and article writing to fiction and how therapeutic that has been!

Merrillee Whren sparked the idea that, even in this day and age, clean romance was marketable.

My critique partners at First Coast Christian Writers, Tracy Redman, Janelle Thomas, Top Noa, Danny Murphy, and Joe Mazerac, read every word of the first draft. Thanks for your friendship, accountability, and encouragement.

My Sister's Keeper
ISBN: 9798691172168
Copyright © 2016 by Dalyn Woods
Cover Illustration & Design: Joseph Mazerac

This is a work of fiction. Names, characters, places, and incidents are either the product of the author's imagination or are used fictitiously. Any resemblance to actual persons, living or dead, business establishments, events, or locales is entirely coincidental.

Scriptures taken from the Holy Bible, New International Version®, NIV®. Copyright © 1973, 1978, 1984, 2011 by Biblica, Inc.™ Used by permission of Zondervan. All rights reserved worldwide. www.zondervan.com The "NIV" and "New International Version" are trademarks registered in the United States Patent and Trademark Office by Biblica, Inc.™

This second edition published by arrangement with Penny Bay Press

 Penny Bay Press

Chapter One

Friday, December 19, 11:00 p.m. – Kidnapped

A burlap hood dropped over Megan Foster's head, shrouding her in darkness. The drawstring, cinched tight, blocked out any remaining illumination from the streetlights. Confusion and disbelief flooded through her.

This can't be happening.

Megan clawed at the fabric, trying to loosen the tightness around her throat, fighting the claustrophobia that threatened to overwhelm her. Calloused hands jerked her arms behind her, crossed and tied her wrists in place. Reality sunk in as she heard a zipping noise and a thin plastic strap dug into her skin.

This is happening, unless I stop it.

Adrenaline pumped through her veins as her fight response kicked into high gear. She broke away, spun, and raised her knee high. She was rewarded with a pain-filled grunt, followed by a string of curses in a thick, unfamiliar accent.

She heard him scramble to his feet, and then his thick hand was around her neck. "Try it again and I'll kill the girl." His sour breath penetrated the mask that kept her from seeing him.

"No," Megan begged, "I'm sorry. Don't hurt Emma. I'll cooperate."

"That's more like it." He shoved her backward.

She stumbled and lost her balance. Blinded by the hood, it felt as if she was falling into a yawning abyss. With hands bound behind her, she tried to slow her momentum, yelping when her sudden landing sent pain shooting up her left arm. Discouragement washed over her. It was ludicrous to think she could overpower this man. Even without the benefit of sight, she could tell he had the physique of an NFL football player. Having utilized the one maneuver she remembered from a self-defense class long ago, she now lay defenseless and at his mercy. Worse, she had angered him, possibly jeopardizing Emma's life.

Her entire body quivered. If she and Emma were to survive this, she had to calm down, to see without her eyes. She forced herself to use her remaining senses. Flattening her hand against the floor, she felt the chill coming from the uncompromising bricks beneath her. Since her toes were backed up against another structure, she gathered they were in a narrow space. An alleyway. That made sense. They had been walking down the sidewalk from the theatre when the men had grabbed them. As hysteria worked to squeeze the air out of her lungs, Megan concentrated on taking slow, deep breaths.

She heard an odd footstep pattern. Step, drag, step, drag. It was too light to be the large man who had charged her. So there were at least two of them, though the second wasn't speaking.

"Stop. You're hurting me." Emma's muffled cries reached Megan, renewing her courage. She had to focus on keeping her sister alive.

"It's okay, Emma. I'm right here," Megan called out.

Her hot breath in the confines of the scratchy cloth nearly suffocated her. She rolled over and crawled toward Emma's voice. The uneven cobblestones dug into her knees.

What do they want?

If robbery was the motive, they would have scored the valuables and been gone. Megan's stomach clenched as a far more sinister purpose came to mind. She braced for the brutal attack, praying that these savages would spare their lives when they were finished with them. How would her fourteen-year-old sister deal with this harsh perversion? She had to give the girl some hope to cling to, something to carry her through the coming ordeal.

"Don't be afraid, Emma. God is always with you."

"No god here," the accented voice snapped as he kicked Megan in the shoulder with such violence her head slammed against the wall.

Excruciating pain tore through her body, leaving a trail of white heat. Drenched in sweat and fighting nausea, Megan curled into a ball on the ground. A terrible moaning filled the air and she silently pleaded for quiet before realizing the sound came from her.

Soft footsteps shuffled toward her and stopped. Rising panic seized Megan as clammy hands lifted her to her feet and propelled her down the corridor. They rounded a corner, and the echoes told her they were now in a large, empty space. Probably an abandoned building. Out of sight, out of hearing, no one would ever find them. Scraping, screeching noises grated on her ears and then she was pushed onto a cold, metal chair.

"Who are you? What do you want?" She choked on the sobs that wracked her body.

A beefy hand walloped her cheek, launching a hundred rockets in her brain. The pain was so intense she barely felt the sharp prick in her thigh, like a bee sting, that sent her into darkness.

Voices came from deep in a tunnel, and Megan roused as unseen hands ripped the mask from her head, turning darkness into blinding light. The suddenness of the action startled her and she tried to scream, but the sound died in her throat. As heat from the lights warmed her, beads of perspiration formed and lazily crawled down her face, creating a maddening desire to scratch. She fought to free her arms but they refused to respond. Dizziness overwhelmed her as the bright lights pulsated in varying colors and intensity.

An odd sensation overtook her as the drug permeated her brain. She seemed to be floating in space, her head detached from her body. Her assailants became nebulous creatures moving along the floor, staging her body. A conversation was taking place. Her mouth moved, but she couldn't hear the words. Fear tightened her stomach and she turned away from the scene.

You told Emma I was always with her. Don't you believe it for yourself?

Megan's fear dissipated and she drifted into peaceful sleep on a soft cloud.

Closing the door, Nathan Harper frowned at the familiar envelope. Another letter. He ripped it open and sorted through the words glued to the page. The different colors and fonts made it difficult to read the individual words cut from the glossy pages of magazines.

Lock and key are together within our grasp. Heat will incinerate your most precious treasure. We'll be watching.

He locked in on *most precious treasure.* Glancing around his minimalist furnishings, he tried to think what possession fit that category. When nothing came to mind, he moved on.

The message made no sense. What could this possibly have to do with military secrets? Opening his desk drawer, he pulled out the folder containing the two previous letters.

Provide the key to Devastation or pay.

That first note had included a return envelope labeled for the courier company that had delivered it. Not knowing what Devastation was and unwilling to involve himself in clandestine activities, Nate had ignored it. A week later the second letter was delivered.

Delay or disclosure will bring Devastation to your love.

Laying the third letter beside the other two, he analyzed them. The new note was longer, but it was missing a key word in the others—Devastation. Still, he was confident it was from the same person. The threat was there in each one—consequences if he reported the notes or failed to act on them. Although he couldn't fathom who or what his *love* or *precious treasure* referred to.

Nate didn't waste time on love, an emotion that only brought grief and torment. He had loved his parents until the death of his mother laid the first stones in his heart. Then, a mere six months later, his father remarried. The betrayal cemented the foundation of an emotional wall. More bitter life experiences had built those early formations into a thick bulwark. After a while, he learned that treating everyone with impassive professionalism kept people at arm's length. No affection equaled no misery.

The only person immune to his defensiveness was the little girl who had won him over as a toddler. She was fourteen now, a fact he had trouble remembering. To him, she was and would always be an innocent child. If he had any treasure here on earth, it would be his half-sister.

Emma.

Grabbing the newest letter, he raced into the darkness. He cranked up his Hummer, peeled out of the driveway, and headed to Jacksonville. Once on the expressway, he ordered Siri to call his friend, private security consultant Paul Spears. When he answered, Nate dove in without preamble. "I got another letter."

"When?"

He glanced at the dashboard clock. "2100. It may not be military secrets they're after."

"I agree. I can't find any reference to code name Devastation. What's this letter say?"

Although the letter sat crumpled on the seat beside him, Nate quoted the message seared on his brain. "I think lock and key reference Megan and Emma. They're spending the weekend in the city."

"Emma. Of course. That's your one Achilles' heel. Who knew they'd be there?"

"Emma was pretty excited. She posted it on Facebook."

"Depending on her privacy settings, the whole world could know."

"That does not encourage me." Nate ground out the words.

"Sorry. What was the other part? Something about heat?"

"Heat will incinerate your most precious treasure." Nate flicked on his blinker as he sped past a slow-moving car on the right.

"Another warning not to go to the police. Where are you now?"

"On my way to the Florida Theater. I've got to be there before the thing ends."

"Be safe, and let me know when you find them."

"Right." Nate ended the call and tossed the phone onto the passenger seat. It landed on the note and he floored the gas.

Nate paced in front of the theatre, waiting for the doors to open. It was a sold-out performance, so he couldn't buy a ticket, and the usher ignored his life-or-death claim. Short of causing a scene and risking arrest, he was relegated to waiting on the sidewalk.

Emma's excitement had crackled through the phone during their call this morning. He could imagine her crooked grin and impish eyes dancing. Every Christmas she looked forward to going to Jacksonville with Megan to see *The Nutcracker*, but she thought this year would be extra special. Nate didn't get the big thrill— something about being fourteen. A girl thing, he supposed.

How long does this show last?

He pulled the note from his pocket and searched for some clue or missed meaning.

Lock and key are together within our grasp. Heat will incinerate your most precious treasure. We'll be watching.

On alert, he glanced around to see if anyone was observing him. A few people entered and exited nearby restaurants, but no one seemed interested in what he was doing.

The note's arrival at 2100 hours gave him little time to make it to the theater. He had to believe the timing was purposeful, allowing no opportunity to strategize or coordinate with the police. Just as well, since Paul concluded that "heat" probably referred to law enforcement.

Nate reflected on his conversation with Paul. If the note was real—and they both believed it was—this would be the perfect place to grab them. They were well-protected on the grounds of the gated estate, and Amelia Island was safe, for the most part. No, the anonymity of the city crowds was where they would make their move. Nate trusted Paul's assessment of the situation.

Paul had been a special agent with Naval Criminal Investigative Services, NCIS, until an accident in the line of duty left him with permanent damage, ending his military career. He took his honorable discharge and struck out on his own. His previous successes and high profile clientele proved he was the best in the business.

They'd had lunch the day after the first note arrived, so Nate had run it by him. After tossing around various scenarios, Paul had offered to come by, run some tests, and do a little digging. When the second note arrived, Paul had again run tests. The results were still pending.

He also encouraged Nate to take the threats seriously, but he had never heard of a mission or weapon called Devastation. Plus, the whole espionage idea seemed implausible. Besides having a reputation for integrity, Nate's job in the Navy didn't give him access to high-level security details. He trained rescue swimmers, an important job he loved, but a long way from spy games. No one in their right mind would think he had or would be willing to sell military secrets. Now he wondered what they were really after and how it involved Megan and Emma.

Nate stuffed the note into his pocket as the doors to the Florida Theatre opened. Throngs of people filled the sidewalks. Most were couples—women in evening dresses, their dates in tuxedoes. They frowned at him as he mingled among them in his jeans, Henley shirt, and tennis shoes. He focused on his mission with little concern for what others thought.

He spotted two women walking away from him together—one short and petite, the other taller and more willowy. The gentle breeze created halos from their identical blonde hair. As he bore down on them, a car pulled up and a man got out, planted a kiss on each of their cheeks, then opened the door and whisked them away.

Nate turned back toward the theatre.

Nothing.

As the crowds thinned, he got back into his Hummer and circled the blocks around the theater. Down Bay, up Forsyth. Caught by a red light, he slammed his fist on the steering wheel. He'd been driving around for an hour. For all he knew, they were tucked safe in bed at the hotel. But he didn't know which one, and no desk clerk was going to give him a room number. Making one last loop through a parking garage, he spotted a lone Volvo on the third floor. Senses on high alert, he got out to investigate closer. Nassau county plates and a Harper Scents parking decal confirmed his suspicion that it was indeed Megan's. Fear struck a deep chord in him. If they were going to walk to the theatre, they would have left their car at the hotel. That could only mean one thing, and it wasn't good. He drove out and parked on the street midway between the garage and the theater and began an alley-by-alley search.

Megan woke with a pounding head and numb arms, but she was free from the plastic ties. The cold of the alley seeped through her thin dress, causing her teeth to chatter. Had it been minutes or hours?

"Emma?" Megan rolled onto her knees and waited for the nausea to subside. After a moment, she tried to stand up, but a rising curtain of darkness threatened to overtake her and she crumpled to the ground. There was no sign of her younger sister. Frantically, she crawled farther down the narrow passage, looking past the dumpster. Fear mingled with the stench of cheap wine, and bile boiled up in her throat. Clawing through the boxes, she uncovered a sleeping vagrant. He gave her an indignant glare before he rolled over and resumed his slumber.

"Emma? Where are you? Emma?" Her voice cracked in her parched throat. She tried standing again, moving gingerly until her foot caught on something in the tangle of trash. She lurched forward, catching herself with her left hand against the alley wall. Pain shot up her arm, and she nursed the swollen wrist. Looking down she realized the strap of her discarded purse had wrapped around her ankle. Relieved, she pulled out her cell phone to call for help. She clicked on the button, and light filled the alley. Then all went dark. *Dead battery.* Tears filled her eyes.

She stumbled toward the deserted street, feeling her way along the building wall until her legs gave way and she staggered and fell. Her bottom hit hard on the concrete, jarring her and sending shards of pain throughout her body. She brushed a lock of hair out of her eyes and discovered a large, sticky goose egg on her forehead. As she drew her hand away, she stared at the blood on it.

"Megan." A familiar male voice rose above the clamor in her head, and she closed her eyes for a second. A towering figure soon appeared at her side. Kneeling down, he gave her a cursory look with gray eyes that contained gold flecks like metal in flint. His blond hair, cut in a buzz, stood at attention like a million little sailors.

Bit by bit relief replaced dread and for a moment, Megan imagined a look of compassion crossed his face. That couldn't be right. Although there was no one more capable in a crisis than Nathan Harper, he held nothing but contempt for her. It made no sense that he would know where she was, let alone rescue her.

"I've been looking for you for two hours."

The weight of her guilt increased. Part of her special surprise for Emma was meeting the cast of the ballet. By the time they left, the theatre crowd had dispersed. If they had left right after the performance, none of this would have happened.

Nate interrupted her thoughts. "Where's Emma?"

Strange, distorted memories came rushing back to her. "I ... I don't know. I've called her..."

"You called her? You didn't even look for her? Right. Your main concern was taking care of yourself."

Ah, that was the Nate she knew. "Of course I looked for her, but she's not there."

The calm exploded. "You let them take her?"

"It happened so fast. I think I was drugged."

He grunted his disapproval and headed down the alley. He rousted the drunk, pulling him up by the scruff of the neck. "There was a teenage girl with this woman. Where is she?"

"Man, I didn't see nothin'." The drunk waved his nearly-full bottle for emphasis.

Nate struck it from his hand, and it shattered on the ground, the clear liquid pooling among the bits of glass.

"Hey, I earned that! I did what the man said."

"So you did see somebody."

"Umm. I might remember if I had a little something to drink."

Nate grabbed the man by the front of the shirt and pinned him against the alley wall. "You'll never drink so much as another drop of water if you don't start talking."

That sobered the drunk. "Tall, skinny guy, well-dressed. Big, burly guy. Bigger than you." He sized up Nate. "Er, well, wider. They came in here with two fine women."

Nate growled.

"No! No! Very nice ladies, dressed real pretty, like they'd been to one of them theatre shows. They weren't the bought kind."

"You got that right. What else?"

"Well, the skinny guy saw me and tossed me some pills. Said they'd give me real nice dreams and when I woke up I'd have a brand new bottle of gin." He looked with longing over Nate's shoulder at the broken bottle. "That's all I know. Really. I fell right asleep, just like he said."

Nate pushed him harder against the wall. "Where's the girl now?"

"I dunno." He pointed toward Megan. "That nosey woman woke me up a minute ago looking for somebody."

Disgusted, Nate dropped him back into the pile of trash and cardboard, then strode down the alley, his face dark as a thundercloud.

"She's been kidnapped. Don't you have an ounce of awareness about your surroundings?" His deep voice bristled with contempt.

Megan tried to rally the strength to argue, to dig out from under the despair that washed over her. She was tired of his constant animosity toward her. The sneer on his face made his opinion of her all too clear. The pounding in her head increased, and she struggled to sit upright. He reached down to steady her, but when he put pressure on her left wrist, she winced.

He lifted her hand, probing the swollen area. Megan flinched as his cool fingers reignited the pain. "No broken bones. I'll bandage that up when we get home."

Home. She shivered at the image the word created. Acceptance and belonging.

Nate mistook her shiver. "Where's your coat? Don't you know it gets cold at night?"

Before she could answer, he scooped her up and carried her down the street to where his Hummer sat on the curb. He dumped her into the passenger seat and tossed her a blanket. "I'm going to find Emma. Don't move." Nate slammed the door.

What a nightmare. She just wanted Emma back by her side, safe and excited about Christmas. The first in their weekend of activities was going to the city for a Friday evening performance of *The Nutcracker*, a formal event. They'd dressed up in their finest. The rumbling in her stomach reminded her they'd missed the next part of their evening—a midnight supper at the River Club, a private restaurant located on the top two floors of a skyscraper. After a stay in a riverfront hotel, they would have spent Saturday shopping. This had become their tradition, a bonding time for sisters. It never occurred to her that muggers would target them.

As Megan huddled under the blanket, groggy and unfocused, she sought comfort in Nate's words even as a sense of foreboding covered her.

He'll find her, he'll find her.

Nate struck out for one last look around for Emma, even though every instinct told him she was gone. As he poked around doorways and alleys, his cell phone rang. He glanced at the caller ID. Paul Spears.

"Speak," Nate said into the phone.

"You were going to call me when you found them."

"Right."

"Nothing?"

"I found Megan. She's sorta roughed up." Nate ran a hand over his buzzed head.

"No sign of Emma?"

"Negative. I'm doing one more sweep. She's smart and strong. She could have gotten away, be hiding somewhere."

"Harper, it's zero two. There's nobody downtown at this hour but the homeless and drunks. If the cops see you, it's going to raise suspicions."

"You're right. I'm headed in." Defeat crashed in on him. It was the kidnapper's move.

"Call me. We'll run scenarios."

"Sure." Nate slipped the phone back onto his belt and headed out of the alley.

A police cruiser turned the corner, and Nate leaned back into the shadows. After it passed he jogged back to the Hummer. The last thing he needed was for the cops to start questioning Megan.

His heart stopped as he approached the vehicle. There was no sign of Megan. Peering in the window, he blew out a breath at the sight of her curled up in a ball, asleep. He slid into the driver's seat.

She stirred beside him. "Did you find her?"

"No." Anger and tension had left him drained.

"You said kidnapped. What aren't you telling me?" Megan's words slurred.

A patrol car eased past, slowing to look them over.

Nate leaned down and placed a finger against her lips. "Not now. Not here. We can't have the cops involved."

Chapter Two

Saturday, December 20, 2:00 a.m.

O nce the police car was gone, Nate jammed the gear stick into drive and turned the vehicle toward I-95. It was a long way back to Amelia Island, providing plenty of time to figure out his next move.

But Megan wasn't about to leave him in peace with his thoughts. Scooting into an upright position, she pounced. "Where are you going? We can't leave until we find Emma."

"There's no finding her. She's gone. Don't you get it yet?"

"That can't..."

"Dad was counting on you to keep her safe, but you were preoccupied with glitz and glamour. You're just like Carol."

"Why do you hate me and Mama so much? What did we ever do...?"

"What did you do?" Nate shook his head. "Carol couldn't wait to dig her claws into Dad's bank account, couldn't wait six months before she was waltzing him down the aisle."

"That's not true. After all Mama had been through, she wanted to wait. George was the one who set the timetable."

Nate knew she was right. He replayed his father's words from that day. "Your mother and I were a great team. She stood by my side as I built this company, and I stood by hers through this horrific disease. I grieved for her suffering, for my loss, for four long years. Now she's home and pain free. I'm still here. I need a companion, a wife. A godly woman is a tremendous help in facing life's daily struggles. I pray you learn this sooner rather than later, son."

"It's been sixteen years and they're still happy. Why can't you accept us?"

Megan, always the peacemaker. He was the one who kept the feud going. Sixteen years since he had dropped out of college, broke all ties with his father, and joined the Navy. Sixteen years of requesting duty stations far away from Florida. Over time his relationship with George Harper had improved, with complete restoration after the birth of Emma. But he wasn't ready to drop his animosity toward Megan yet. "You didn't like me any better—wouldn't even look at me that day."

Megan averted her eyes, scratching at a stain on her dress. "I was nervous. The formal gown, the high heels ... I was terrified I'd fall flat on my face and ruin the ceremony." Giving up on the stain, she scrutinized him. "And you, you were kinda intimidating. So stoic and, and tall. You're very tall."

"I was trying to wrap my mind around what was going on. I come home for Christmas break and Dad announces he's getting married? We had just buried my mother in June."

"We can't change the past, but can't we call a truce for Emma's sake?"

He refused to flinch under Megan's stare. Instead, he gripped the steering wheel tighter and focused straight ahead.

Megan sighed, dropped her head back on the headrest and closed her eyes.

Against his better judgment, he glanced her way. With bare feet and her stained and torn dress, she didn't look like the stuck-up debutante he remembered. She had a goose egg on her forehead. Mascara smudged with blood and dirt around puffy eyes gave her the appearance of a sailor after a Saturday night brawl. Her hair was shorter, curving around her chin, yet it remained the perfect shade of blonde. She was still petite, her heart-shaped face delicate. The vulnerability in her blue eyes had rallied his protective nature. He compensated by attacking her, his usual *modis operandi* for stifling his emotions. He admired her for fighting back, but now she lay in the seat, eyes closed, face drained of color, and he felt guilty for his harshness.

They were crossing the county line, only a few more miles to the island and then home. He hadn't realized how tense he was until he relaxed. A black SUV sat on the side of the road, and Nate changed lanes out of courtesy to the stranded motorist. As he passed, headlights popped on and the SUV moved into traffic.

Coincidence?

Megan's eyes fluttered open and she spoke, breaking his reverie. "We should file a missing person report. Start an Amber alert."

The pleading in her eyes seemed genuine, so he looked away, focusing on the road ahead. Their trip down memory lane had raised old resentments that he found hard to squash. Despite her claims of nerves and timidity, he chose to stick to his version of events. The last thing he was going to do was let the little princess wheedle him into caving on his position.

"No ma'am. My mission, my rules."

Megan grew more animated, swiveling in her seat to face him. "Nate, we need the police, the FBI, whoever can find her. This isn't some Hollywood action movie."

"My only concern is Emma's safety." Focused on the rearview mirror, Nate had no interest in an argument. He moved to the inside lane and watched as three cars back, the black SUV changed as well.

Odd, but not conclusive.

"Me, too, but I'm not going along with your rebel mentality." Her voice rose as she became more passionate.

"We'll discuss it later." He slowed to just below the speed limit while other cars whipped past him on the right. The SUV started to gain and then also slowed, matching his speed.

Megan continued her plea. "Every minute counts. The sooner they start looking, the better chance they have of finding her before..."

He saw his opening, swerved over three lanes, and careened down the exit ramp. He slammed on brakes at the bottom and watched as the suspect vehicle moved over one lane and crossed the overpass above them.

"Are you crazy? What are you doing?"

Nate pulled the note out of his pocket and thrust it in her face.

Megan took it from him and read it out loud. "Lock and key are together within our grasp. Heat will incinerate your most precious treasure. We'll be watching." Her eyes narrowed. "What does it mean?"

"It means we're not calling the police. End of discussion."

Megan slumped down in her seat, and Nate turned right onto A1A. He regretted his shortness with her, but he didn't dare go against the kidnapper's wishes. He searched for reasons that someone would be following them. The most obvious was the kidnapper verifying that they hadn't contacted the cops. Or perhaps they wanted to know they were home to receive the ransom demand. Only three people knew about the threats.

He stopped at a red light, and his eyes slid sideways for a glimpse of Megan in the seat next to him. She flexed her fingers and rubbed her swollen wrist. He had to admit, she was holding up rather well. Maybe she was tougher than he assumed. He shook off the notion. He had built a wall on the foundation of his initial impressions and he wasn't ready to tear it down.

Her bowed head allowed a blonde curtain to hide her face. His fingers itched to tuck the strands behind her ear, assure her of his protection. His defense mechanism wasn't working.

Forcing his eyes back to the road, he crossed the bridge onto the island and turned off the highway into The Dunes, a neighborhood of oceanfront estates where his father lived with his wife Carol and their daughter, Emma. Megan occupied the guest cottage on the grounds. His father preferred to keep the gates of the estate open. In light of tonight's events, that would have to change immediately. As Nate pulled into the driveway, a black SUV swung in behind him and focused a spot light on the Hummer.

"Megan, stay put." Nate eased out of the truck, avoiding any sudden moves.

Slamming the door, the passenger strode toward Nate, stopping mere inches from him. "Where're you going in such a hurry?"

"Who are you?" Nate asked.

"Frank Silva, AIPD," he said, opening his bomber jacket to reveal a badge.

Cops. How had they found out so quickly?

An older man, dressed in a three-piece suit, rounded the front of the vehicle, hand extended to Nate. "Maurice Benoit, Amelia Island Police Department. I apologize for my partner's exuberance. We're looking for an Emma Harper."

"I'm Nathan Harper. What's this about?"

Hearing the Hummer's passenger door open, he willed Megan to keep inside and stay quiet. But Megan had never done his bidding.

"Nate?" She leaned out the door, shielding her eyes. "What's going on?"

"Emma Harper?" Silva asked, dark eyes flashing.

Megan stumbled out of the Hummer and rushed toward the detective. "What? What about Emma?"

"She's not here?" Benoit asked.

Nate stepped forward and placed an arm around Megan, drawing her to his side. "As you can see, Detective, we just arrived home, so we can't really say if she's here or not."

"Do you expect her to be here?"

Nate weighed his words. "I expect her to be in Jacksonville. She went to see *The Nutcracker* with a friend, and they were going to spend the weekend in the city."

Shuffling his feet, Benoit bent his silver head to review his notes. "Have you heard from her tonight, say, since eleven?"

Megan squirmed at his side, a quiet whimper escaping from her.

Nate gripped her tighter. "What's this about?" Had someone witnessed the kidnapping? He struggled to keep his face blank, eager to know the identity of the kidnappers, but anxious that this encounter with the police could jeopardize Emma's safety.

"The Jacksonville Sheriff's Office found her student ID in an alley downtown, near the theatre district," Benoit said.

"Just her ID? No wallet or purse?" Nate tried to sound concerned without giving anything away.

"They also reported a suspicious vehicle in the vicinity." The stocky-built Silva aimed his flashlight at Nate's face, before moving it to the Hummer parked in the driveway. "Very similar to yours."

Ignoring Silva's cockiness, Nate looked back at his truck. "There're a few of these around." If the ID was in the alley where the girls were kidnapped, it meant nothing. But if it was in a different alley... Could Emma have escaped? He should have looked longer. He needed to find out the information without alerting the cops to the fact that she was missing.

Before he could formulate a plan, Detective Silva took a different tactic.

"Getting home kinda late." Silva spoke to Nate as he studied Megan's bedraggled appearance.

Nate shrugged. "It's Friday night, holiday season. Lots of parties."

"You don't look dressed for a party."

Nate stared him down. "It was a casual evening."

Silva raised his eyebrows as he looked from Megan back to Nate.

"She likes dressing up. Me and you, not so much," Nate said with a nod toward Detective Silva's jeans.

Dismissing the comment, Silva turned to Megan. "Ma'am, is there something you'd like to say?"

Megan shook her head and looked up at Nate. "We should call Emma."

Silva stepped a little closer and lowered his voice. "You don't have to be afraid. We can protect you. Come over here and explain your injuries."

Megan shook her head. "I fell, hit my head. It's embarrassing, really, but I'm fine."

Benoit spoke to Nate. "Let's move up here, and you can tell me more about this party."

Nate avoided eye contact with Megan, knowing the two detectives would pick up on any signals sent between them. He pretended to cooperate and hoped that Megan would keep her cool. "Sure, detective."

Megan clung to his arm. "I don't feel well. Can't we just go in?"

"If that's what you want." Nate patted her hand on his arm.

"You don't have to cover for him," Silva said as he reached for Megan.

"Look, she explained. I didn't beat her up. She doesn't want to press charges. I'd really like to go inside and call Emma."

"We'd like to listen in on that call."

"No."

Benoit looked taken aback. "No?"

"Guys, with all due respect, it's late and we're tired. I'm going to get her cleaned and doctored, call Emma, and then we're going to bed."

Megan coughed, and Nate rubbed her back sympathetically.

Silva pressed a business card into Megan's hand. "You can call us anytime."

Benoit gave Nate a hard look. "Have Emma drop by the station and pick up her ID."

Nodding, Nate prayed Emma would be able to do that soon.

Nate raised his hand in a salute as the SUV backed out of the driveway. As soon as they were out of sight, he released Megan and strode into the house.

Megan chased after him, his long legs moving him faster than she could keep up. The effects of the drug were wearing off, and adrenaline pumped through her system. "Those detectives had Emma's ID, and you acted as if nothing was going on.

Furthermore, you had me doing the same. You want to clue me in?"

Nate turned and walked away from her, fueling her anger.

"We weren't random victims tonight. Emma was targeted, and you knew it was going to happen. Care to explain that?"

"The note I showed you arrived at 2100 hours."

Megan scrunched her face as she subtracted twelve from twenty-one. "So, at nine o'clock you got a note about locks and keys and treasures burning up?" She stared at him, eyes narrowed.

Nate dropped a folder onto the kitchen counter. "The first one arrived two weeks ago. The second one came a week later."

Megan opened the folder. Straight out of an 80s television drama, the letter was comprised of words cut out of a magazine. It contained a vague demand for information, a riddle. It made no sense to Megan. It seemed surreal, but the agitation radiating from Nate as he paced in front of the French doors forced her to face reality. Emma was in serious danger.

The second letter demanded the key to Devastation.

"What's Devastation?"

Nate turned sharply. "Don't you know?"

Megan wracked her brain. "No, I've never heard of it."

"It must be some perfume you and Dad created. They always have bizarre names like that."

"Did you ask George about it? Tell him about these letters?"

Nate shook his head. "The letters were sent to me. I was researching Navy ops for a connection. Even showed it to a former NCIS agent. It wasn't until tonight that I considered a tie to Harper Scents."

Megan moved into the family room, carrying the folder with her. Her head pounded and she felt unsteady on her feet. Sinking onto the sofa, she closed her eyes for a moment and willed the dizziness away. When she opened her eyes, Nate was sitting in the chair facing her.

"When I found you like..." he waved a hand in her direction "...and Emma was gone, I knew they had taken her."

"What do they want?" she murmured to herself as she skimmed the letters for a clue.

Nate crossed an ankle over his knee. "They'll contact us once they've ascertained the police aren't here."

Heat rose in Megan, and she jumped up from the sofa. "How can you be so calm?"

"Losing my cool isn't going to help Emma."

"Losing your cool? We've lost Emma!" Megan clenched her fists by her side.

"You need to control your emotions, as well."

His words ignited a bomb in her head, turning the world red just before darkness enveloped her.

Nate moved with lightning speed as Megan swayed. Her eyes rolled back, and she collapsed in his arms. He eased her down onto the sofa, noting the white pallor beneath the red flush of her anger. When he returned with the first-aid kit, her eyes were open but heavy lidded. She presented all the signs of a concussion.

As Megan dug her elbows into the sofa in an effort to sit up, Nate stopped her, placing a hand on her shoulder and an ice pack on her forehead. "Hey, you've had a rough night. Let's save round three for in the morning."

She grimaced as she took the ice pack from him. "Everything's so jumbled."

"It'll clear up in a few hours with rest." He examined her more closely than he had done in the alley. A mixture of mud and blood marred the pale-pink color of her evening dress. A jagged tear in the hem revealed cuts and scrapes on her knees. He removed an antiseptic wipe from the first aid kit and went to work. When she tensed, he lightened his touch.

By the time Nate had cleaned her wounds, exhaustion had taken its toll and Megan was sound asleep. He pulled an afghan over her, sat back on the coffee table, and stared at her.

Even beaten and dirty, she made his insides hum. Her femininity left him susceptible to feelings he had fought to cover only to have them laid open again every time they met. But he wasn't interested in a physical attraction. He needed someone he could respect and trust enough to lower his defenses. He wasn't sure what that looked like, but it couldn't be Megan. He had always equated her beauty with a haughty, selfish attitude. When she greeted him with soft-spoken kindness, it brought out the worst in him.

Tonight he saw a glint of determination in her as she argued for calling the police. It was the first time he had ever heard her raise her voice or disagree with anyone. Although pride kept him from admitting he wasn't sure what the better strategy was, the fact that she would stand up to him to protect Emma intrigued him. Maybe she had more substance than he had seen. One thing they did agree on—Emma's safety was paramount.

Long ago he had vowed Emma would never be helpless or weak, like Megan and Carol. For her birthday, he had taken her to a rock wall for climbing lessons. Now he wished he had taken her to a shooting range and taught her to defend herself. But Emma was tough. She never backed down from a challenge. Wherever she was, he knew she had an inner strength that would carry her through until he could find her.

"Lord, help me make wise decisions."

Now what? Nate refused to stand by and do nothing while waiting for the kidnappers to contact him. He pulled his phone from his belt, glanced at the time—0500—punched the contacts icon, and selected a number. Paul Spears must have been expecting his call, because he answered without greeting.

"Any contact?"

Nate wandered out onto the patio, closing the French door behind him. "Nothing yet. You were right, though. JSO made me coming out of the alley. And what's worse, they found Emma's student ID."

"Harper, that's not good. The kidnappers might be watching your place. You gotta keep the cops away."

"Yeah, well, bad news. Amelia Island PD greeted us at the gate."

"So a couple of uniforms showed up to return the ID? That's nothing to worry about."

"No, detectives. Silva and Benoit. They were kinda intense, and I'm not sure my story convinced them." Nate glanced through the glass to be sure Megan was still sleeping.

"I'll be in the office around nine. I can place a call under the guise of getting some information. Just let them know somebody's on it. They'll back off."

"Let's wait on that. These guys are small town and bored. If they sense there is a case, they may start digging around on their own. I'll let you know if they come back. Besides, they already want to string me up for domestic violence. Let's not give them the idea to add kidnapping to the charge."

Chapter Three

Saturday, December 20, 8:00 a.m. – Ransom Demand

Sunlight danced across Megan's sleep-laden eyelids. After fighting unsuccessfully to open them, her attention turned to her throbbing head. She reached up and fingered the tender knot on her forehead. Slowly the events of the previous evening came back to her.

Emma! She had to find Emma.

She sat straight up then grabbed her head in both hands, as if holding still would stop the parade marching through it.

"Megan?"

She heard Nate's deep voice and had a hazy memory of him waking her every time she drifted into a blessed sleep. Had she verbalized her unkind thoughts at the intrusions into her silent and dark cocoon? Mortified, she opened her eyes to find Nate staring at her, an odd expression on his handsome face.

Ugh, I must look terrible.

She wiped her hands across her crumpled, dusty-rose dress and eased her feet onto the floor. Taking in her surroundings, she realized she was on the couch in the family room of the main house.

Nate leaned forward with his elbows resting on his knees, coffee cup cradled in his hands.

She turned from his intense stare. Some caffeine and a shower would help her get her bearings, and then she'd be able to look for Emma. It was obvious Nate wasn't going to do anything.

"Could I get some of that coffee?" Her voice squeaked, and she flinched in response.

Nate didn't answer, but he set down his cup and disappeared into the kitchen.

Megan stood and the room swirled around her. She plopped back onto the sofa. When she looked up, Nate stood in the doorway. She was mortified he had witnessed her unladylike descent. After that display, he wasn't going to let her out of his sight. Although that didn't matter since she wouldn't get much searching done if she couldn't even stand up for five seconds. Her eyes stung with unshed tears of frustration.

"Eat some food." He set a bowl of grits with crumbled bacon on the side table along with a glass of orange juice.

"Coffee?" She croaked again.

"Brewing." He pointed to the food. "Eat."

She didn't think she was hungry, but the smell of fresh bacon was too tempting to pass up. By the time Nate disappeared and returned again with a mug and pot of coffee, she'd finished off the last bite. The headache was beginning to resolve, and she was starting to feel human again. She tucked her leg underneath her and covered herself with an afghan. Then she curled her hands around the warm coffee cup Nate handed her.

He tossed her the remote. "Watch some TV. I've got work to do."

"I can help..." She sat forward but closed her eyes against the dizziness.

"Sit tight. Doctor's orders." He strode from the room.

Megan set her cup on the side table and leaned forward until her head was between her knees.

Nate had every right to be angry with her. She was responsible for Emma's kidnapping. How would she ever face Mama and George?

It was her fault Daddy left. Her fault Mama had struggled to make ends meet. Her fault Emma was gone, and now it would be her fault when George disowned her as well. She gasped for air.

Pressing her fingers against her temples, she willed herself to relive the events. The smells and sounds were all vivid in her mind, but nothing seemed a significant clue. If only she had been more observant or fought harder, Emma would be safe now. She shook her head. This blame game was getting her nowhere.

Megan swallowed the last drop of coffee then tested her legs, waiting for the spinning to return. When it didn't, she eased down the hall to the powder room, where she stood in front of the mirror and surveyed her appearance. Her face was white and washed out. Black smudges around her eyes made her look like a raccoon. She wet a washcloth, spritzed it with a little soap, and washed her face. After all the mascara was removed, only the greenish yellow around the bump on her forehead remained. She washed her hands and noticed the thin abrasions surrounding her wrists. A shudder ran through her. Not wanting to dwell on it, she found some toothpaste in a closet and scrubbed her teeth with her finger then rinsed her mouth. Her teeth still didn't feel clean, and she longed for a change of clothes. Eager to have a proper shower, she left the bathroom intending to dash across the lawn to her cottage. But as she stepped out of the powder room, her legs turned to rubber and she almost didn't make it back to the couch. Hygiene would have to wait.

Nate set about cleaning the galley, using the mundane task to clear his head and refocus. He'd spent a restless night cramped up in the recliner, waking every two hours to rouse Megan, according to field medic protocol. Thankfully, her injuries were minor, but she still suffered from the concussion, which would limit a rapid response if the kidnappers made a ransom demand. He also suspected Megan would continue her campaign to call in law enforcement, and he'd have to keep a close eye on her to make sure she didn't do so behind his back.

He finished the last of the dishes and wiped down the counters. Satisfied that the kitchen was spic and span, he strolled into the family room, where Megan slept on the couch. She must have washed up, because the mascara smudges around her eyes were gone. Without makeup she appeared younger, more vulnerable.

Get a grip. Now is not the time to pursue this.

He pulled the afghan over Megan's legs, dropping it at the bow that marked her tiny waist. As if covering her could bury his emotions.

He strode into his father's office, determined to find some clue about Devastation. The more information he had before the kidnapper contacted him, the more negotiating power he would have. He rummaged through the papers on the desk and then checked the drawers.

Unsuccessful, he tested the file drawers of the credenza. Locked. *No problem.* He pulled out his pocket knife and jiggled the lock until it opened, then perused one file after another. Turned out his father was sentimental. The folder labeled *Nate* contained school awards and pictures—a reminder of the skinny geek he was before he set about changing his image by working out and bulking up.

He found his certificate of baptism, along with pictures from church camp, where he'd made his father's faith his own. He'd had spiritual ups and downs, along with growth spurts intermingled with periods of apathy. Dark days of doubt had followed the accident, but then healing had begun. Today, he was satisfied with his spiritual status. The men on his crew respected his faith and admired his convictions.

So what are you hiding from?

"I'm not hiding," he argued out loud with his conscience.

What about Megan?

"What about her?" He glanced over his shoulder, embarrassed to be talking to himself. He started to close the drawer of memories when an envelope with his name scrawled on it caught his eye. Opening it, he found a letter from his father.

Dear Son,

I have enclosed a portion of my last will and testament drawn up a short while ago.

He had reconciled his mother's death. He wasn't prepared to contemplate his father's demise. But he forced himself to read on.

In the event of my death, my son, Nathan Harper, and my step-daughter, Megan Foster, will run Harper Scents jointly. Nate will be in charge of administration, finance, and marketing. Megan will head up research, development, and production. The shares of the company are to be divided four ways, between the two aforementioned, my wife Carol, and our daughter, Emma. The company, in part or in whole, and any shares of said company are not to be sold until Emma reaches the age of twenty-one and can make an informed decision about her future as it pertains to the company. In the event that Carol and I die before Emma reaches majority age, guardianship shall be shared jointly with Nathan Harper and Megan Foster.

"I'll honor your wishes then, but that's a long time away." Nate crumpled the letter and tossed it onto the desk before he moved on to the next file. He tried to concentrate, but his focus was broken. He snatched up the crumpled letter, flattened it out, and continued reading.

Nate, I urge you to put aside your animosity toward Megan. As you can see, in the future, you and Megan will be working together very closely, and I would like the two of you to have an amicable relationship before the stresses of running a company take their toll.

I don't want to break confidences, but suffice it to say that Megan had a troubled childhood and has worked hard to overcome those obstacles. I know you can understand that struggle, as you have made great strides in wrestling with your own demons. I'm proud of the man you have become. This acrimony you bear toward Megan is not who you are. I pray that you will humble yourself and ask for Megan's forgiveness.

"Ask Megan for forgiveness. That's rich." He stuffed the letter back into the file and slammed the drawer shut. "The little princess has outflanked you, Dad."

Megan didn't know how long she had slept, but her headache was gone. She sat up and the room didn't spin. Then she realized that the soft melody of her ringtone had woken her. She looked around and saw no sign of Nate. She snatched her phone from the coffee table and eased out the French doors to the pool area.

Caller ID showed it was Sonia Kaufmann, the corporate attorney for Harper Scents. Her sunny personality was a bright spot among the serious-minded introverts Megan worked with on a daily basis. Over the past year and a half since Sonia had joined the firm, she and Megan had become close friends.

"Hey girl!" Sonia's cheerful voice danced across the line.

"How's the skiing?" Megan cleared her scratchy throat.

"Great! We had a fresh coat of powder last night. I've been on the slopes since the lift opened. How was the ballet? Emma having a good time?"

Megan tried to carry off a normal conversation. "Yeah, great."

"You don't sound like you're having fun."

An idea formed. "Say, I've got a random question. If the company were to need a large sum of money on short notice, and say there was a long weekend or holiday approaching…"

Sonia interrupted her with a chuckle. "Just how much shopping have you and Emma done this weekend?"

"We may have gone a little overboard." Megan forced a lighthearted laugh. "But seriously, are there any liquid funds for an emergency?"

"Sorry doll, you'll have to ask the finance boys. What's going on?"

"My overactive imagination, that's all."

"You don't sound good. Spill it."

"No. It's fine. It's gonna be fine. Tell me about your trip."

Making appropriate noises as needed, she half-listened to Sonia as she told one story after another of adventures on the slopes and shopping in the quaint, winter village. Megan loved her friend's enthusiasm, but today she couldn't wait to get her off the phone. Finally, her co-worker ran out of stories.

"Sounds like you're having a great time. I'll see you after the holidays. Merry Christmas." Megan pressed the end button and leaned her head back against the stone wall of the house.

Oh, Emma.

Nate's stomach grumbled, bringing him back to the present. He stood up and stretched, flexing the muscles that had stiffened in his shoulders from leaning over the files. He wandered into the kitchen as Megan came in from the pool patio. She spotted him, and an odd look crossed her face.

What's she up to? "I'm fixing some lunch," he told her as he headed into the kitchen.

"I'm really not hungry." She followed him.

Biting his tongue, he opened the refrigerator and pulled out a steak.

"Shouldn't we be looking for Emma?"

He handed her a container of yogurt. "Isn't this what women like you eat?"

Her bright eyes dulled, and he regretted his brusqueness. She loved Emma as much as he did. That much they did agree on. He softened his voice. "We're at their mercy, their timetable."

"That doesn't sound like the conquering hero."

Impatience flooded him, but before he spoke out in anger, he remembered his father's letter. *Play nice.* He ran a hand over his buzz cut. "We need a target before we can plan or execute the mission."

Megan sat at the kitchen bar and set the yogurt aside. "I don't have access to company money. The accounting department handles that. The whole company shuts down for Christmas vacation, so I don't even know if I can contact anyone. There may be a little bit of cash in the safe, but nothing close to the amount a kidnapper would demand."

He looked up from the steak he was searing, surprised at her logical assessment of the situation. Anticipating demands and working on a solution. Just like him.

"Megan, it's not your job. I'll get Emma back."

"But it is. Don't you see?" She ran her hands across the manila folder containing the three notes. "I think Emma is the lock and I'm the key. They want something from me."

Nate rounded the bar. He and Spears had come to the same conclusion. He stood behind her, not knowing what to do.

Comfort her.

He hesitated to act on his conscience's instructions.

A knock at the front door saved him from his dilemma. When he answered, a college-aged boy dressed in a delivery uniform greeted him. Megan raced around Nate and snatched the letter from the courier's hand while he signed. When he turned, Megan had slumped to the floor, her face colorless. Not waiting to see what the note contained, he sped out the door and grabbed the messenger as he was getting into his car. Nate slammed him against the hood.

"Who are you?" He twisted the boy's coat under his chin.

The kid shrank back.

"Who hired you?" Nate shouted again and added a shake to the twist.

"I ... I don't know. I'm just making deliveries."

Of course he was. Nate released the kid, disgusted with himself. "Sorry," he mumbled and headed back to the house.

When he entered the foyer, the letter was on the floor at Megan's feet. He picked it up. Varying colors and fonts of letters cut from magazines formed the message:

72 hours for Devastation or the lock gets blown. Video at 10 p.m.

Chapter Four

"Megan."

She looked at Nate with wide blue eyes.

"What is Devastation?"

She blinked.

He knelt beside her and gently shook her shoulder. "Think, Megan. Where does Dad keep the formulas?"

She roused and stumbled to her feet, clutching his arms with a steel grip. "We don't make anything called Devastation."

"They think you do. There has to be something. Maybe you just don't know about it."

She spun away from him. "The safe at the office. That's where anything of value is kept."

Nate followed her out the door. She tried to climb into the Hummer, still wearing the dirty, torn evening dress that drove him to distraction. *Maybe it's the color.* "Don't you want to change your clothes?" he asked as he gave her a lift up.

She shook her head. "No time. C'mon."

He released her to the passenger seat and rounded the front of the vehicle, glad she hadn't mentioned calling the police. He sped toward the corporate offices of Harper Scents.

Once there, Megan used a keypad combination and thumbprint recognition to gain access to the building, elevator, and executive offices.

As she ran down the long hallway, he had no trouble keeping pace with her. His long stride matched two of hers. "Do you have the combination to the safe?"

"Me and George … the only ones." She panted but kept moving.

When they reached George's office, she brought out a folding stool from behind the file cabinet and set it up under a landscape oil painting. Sliding the painting aside revealed a safe, and she again used a keypad combination and thumbprint recognition to open it.

He came up behind her and peered over her shoulder. There was some cash, a couple of perfume bottles, and a large binder.

Megan pulled out the thick notebook. "These are all the formulas Harper Scents uses." She passed it to him.

He laid it on the desk and flipped it open. "It's gibberish. What's this? Some kind of code?"

Megan nodded. "George loves puzzles, so he uses them to protect the proprietary blends. For the exclusive Harper Scents, three to four chemists are involved in the manufacturing process. They each get a portion of the formula. They work in separate rooms, and George destroys the instructions when they're finished."

"Are you saying my dad's paranoid?"

She nodded. "With good reason." Megan stepped off the stool and moved toward the desk. "If a corporate spy got hold of these, it could wipe out the business."

"Perfume. We're talking about perfume, aren't we?"

"Not the run-of-the-mill stuff. The designer market is *very* competitive." She ran her finger down the alphabetical tabs and stopped at D. When she turned the pages, two envelopes fell out. Megan ripped into the envelope marked Devastation and read out loud.

Dear Nate and Megan:

Devastation is a very special formula, in that it will change both your lives forever. And so I will not give it to you. Instead, you must work for it. And not only that, but you must work in partnership with each other. I have recently given you each a gift, and in those gifts lie the puzzles. The answers to one puzzle will provide clues to the second puzzle, which in turn will spell out the answer to the third puzzle.

Your individual strengths complement one another, and a partnership of this kind will prove that together your potential is exponentially greater than separate.

I have named this formula Devastation, but my hope is that by working together, the outcome will be Harmonious.

Nate picked up the second envelope and frowned at the label. "Last Will and Testament?"

"Why would that be in the formula book?" Megan asked.

"Let's check the intel." His eyes skimmed the page, skipping the part he had read in his dad's office. "Ah. Here's the interesting part."

To my son Nate and my step-daughter Megan, I have left the formula for Devastation, my greatest achievement to date. I believe the value of this will exceed that of even Chanel No. 5.

"That's motive." He leaned on the desk.

"But we don't have the formula, and I can't think when George gave me a gift—other than my birthday."

Nate pulled out his phone and punched the keys.

"Who are you calling?"

"I'm not wasting time on stupid games. Dad can give us the formula." He heard two rings and then a click. He looked at the phone and dialed again with the same results. "The call won't go through. Try Carol."

"Good idea." She placed the call and hit the speaker button.

"Hello."

"Mama! I'm so glad you ans—"

"This is Carol Harper," the recording continued.

"Ugh."

"Please leave a message after the tone."

"Mama, call me as soon as you get this message. It's very important." Megan punched the end key and stared at Nate. "Why can't we reach them?"

"Their phones are turned off." He sighed. "At least you got voicemail."

"Yes, but will they check it?"

Nate didn't want to explore that scenario. "Try sending a text."

"Okay, but then I'm calling the cruise line. There must be a way to get hold of passengers in an emergency."

"Good idea." Her logic surprised him.

It took Megan a few minutes to send the text and then look up the number for the cruise line. She hit the speaker key when the customer service representative answered the phone.

"Yes, I'm trying to get in touch with a passenger. There's been an emergency at home, and I need to talk to them."

"Certainly. I'll be glad to help you with that. What's the passenger's name?"

"It's a couple. George and Carol Harper."

"Thank you. I can relay your message to their stateroom. Oh, I'm sorry. What was the name again?"

"George and Carol Harper," Megan repeated.

"Are you sure they sailed with Festival Cruise Line?"

Megan clenched her fists. "They left out of Jacksonville on Thursday for five days on the Fiesta Festival."

"Let me double check. No, I'm sorry. We don't show them on the manifest."

"Thank you." Nate ended the call.

Megan sank onto the sofa. "Where could they be?"

"Don't panic. We can figure this out. Dad gave me a Sudoku book the other day, but..." He spoke to an empty room, because Megan disappeared. As he pushed off the desk to look for her, she reappeared, puzzle book in hand.

"He gave me one the other day too. I didn't think about it, because he gives them to me all the time." She looked at Nate and then averted her eyes. "I like to work them on my lunch hour." She flipped through the book and stopped near the middle. "Here it is— Megan's Puzzle." She turned the book toward him so he could see it. "And look, it's a jumble with a puzzle inside the puzzle, like the instructions said, but no clues. That makes it hard."

"Mine must be the first puzzle that provides the clues to the second puzzle," Nate said.

"So where is it?"

"At my house. I'll drop you off first."

"Oh, no you don't. The instructions are for us to work this together."

A ragamuffin shouldn't be so adorable. He resisted the image with gruffness. "You'll change clothes first, or AIPD will have me up on abuse charges."

"Far be it from me to ruin your precious image." She proceeded down the hall toward the elevator.

Maybe it was the bare feet. Whatever it was, he had an overwhelming instinct to pick her up and carry her. Instead, he followed her into the elevator.

The ride home passed with both lost in their own thoughts. Nate drove through the gates of the estate, past the portico of the main house, and onto the gravel drive that led to the cottage that sat on a bluff overlooking the Atlantic Ocean.

Megan opened the truck door and slid to the ground before he had the Hummer in park.

He sauntered in behind her, expecting a long delay. But he had made the demand, so he'd suffer the consequences.

He remembered the cottage from growing up. The dark hardwood floors contrasted with the white bead board built-ins. He braced for a barrage of pillows, candles, and frou-frou. Instead, it had an uncluttered warmth. Decorated, but not over the top. Overall, the furnishings were white with a few light blues and greens for color. He had expected high end, but the pieces had a homey touch. It exuded a clean, fresh, airy feel and the floors and built-ins remained the same. She had surprised him again.

Megan shut her bedroom door, relieved to be alone with her frightening thoughts. The events of the last few hours had been like a car wreck where everything moves in slow motion until the jarring stop slams one into the steering wheel. Somehow she had hoped Emma would come strolling through the door and it would all be a misguided teenaged prank.

The note eliminated that possibility.

She tugged off her dress, trading it for an ivory pair of jeans and wiggled into a sea-green, knit shirt. Ducking into the bathroom, she ran a toothbrush around her mouth and flicked a comb through her fine, blonde hair. She draped a side part of bangs across her forehead to disguise the swelling, plastering it with hairspray to avoid its return. Satisfied that her appearance wouldn't cause Nate's arrest for assault and battery, she slipped on a pair of sandals and returned to the living room.

She found him studying the books and pictures on her shelves. He turned to face her, examining her from head to toe like one of his troops on parade.

"C'mon." He opened the front door and motioned to her.

She took that to mean she had passed inspection and hurried by him. However, the effects of the concussion lingered, and a wave of dizziness struck her. She swayed against him, and he grabbed her arm to steady her. The sheer bulk of him was comforting. Until he spoke.

"You should stay here. You're not up to this," he said with a grunt.

Refusing to let him see how his words stung, she jutted her chin and willed her head to stop spinning. "I'm going with you."

Their eyes remained locked for a few seconds before Nate broke the contact and pulled her toward the Hummer. She wasn't sure why he relented and let her win their battle of wills, but she was glad he did and determined that she wouldn't be a hindrance.

After crossing the intra-coastal waterway, they rode in silence down the two-lane road that traversed the creeks, marshes, and hammocks as they headed for the main land. Megan stared out the window, where centuries-old live oak trees stretched their arms across the road, creating a tunnel of shade dappled with sunlight.

She couldn't concentrate on the beauty. Remembering her own terror, the strange visions that she assumed were drug-induced, she imagined how frightened Emma must be. Had they drugged her as well? She rubbed her wrist and wondered if her sister had injuries that needed attention. Shivering at the thought of Emma in some cold, dark place, Megan wiped a tear from her eye. Was she safe? Was she hungry?

She thought of Nate trying to make her stay home and her anger flared. Yes, she was jealous of the affection he showed Emma. It made her feel that much more of an outsider in her own family. But she was willing to put aside her feelings to save their half-sister. He could at least do the same. They should be working as a team. Emma's life depended on it.

As they waited for the ferry that would take them across the river, she pondered his dismissal of her. The more she thought, the more she fumed. She'd offered olive branches over the years to no avail. Not this time.

"Did you really think you could leave me behind?"

"Any doctor—"

"Don't pretend you're protecting me. You're trying to get me out of the way. Did you ever stop to consider that I might be a valuable asset? I'm intelligent with good problem-solving skills. George sees it. He trusts me."

Nate concentrated on traversing the narrow plank that linked the dock to the ferry. "So I've heard—double major in botany and chemistry. You're quite the overachiever, and here I am, nothing but a squid. No wonder he's turning half the company over to you— you're everything a father could want."

"Here's a news flash—George would rather leave all of Harper Scents to his son, but you turned your back on him. How dare you cast me as the conniving Jacob stealing your Esau's birthright?"

The deckhand waved them into position, and Megan couldn't escape the confines of the vehicle fast enough. The argument left her shaking. As a rule, she avoided confrontations like the plague, but Emma's needs trumped her discomfort. She was determined to save her sister, and she'd fight anyone who tried to stop her.

She strolled across the deck and leaned over the railing, its cold steel a balm to her inner pain. The screaming caws of the seagulls assaulted her ears as they swooped down to pluck lunch from the water. Groaning and lurching as it broke free of its moorings, the ferry began its lumbering journey. A manatee, bearing battle scars of previous encounters with boat propellers, spiraled over in the water to escape the wake formed by the large vessel.

You and me, sister, constantly dodging weapons of men.

As a child, alcohol and harsh words had driven her into the shadows, leaving scars of insecurity and worthlessness. She still battled self-recrimination, but in this instance it was justified.

She watched as shrimp boats lined up, their rigging towering over the small fishing village across the river. The smell of fish mingled with the clean salt air as the breeze picked up. Megan grabbed at strands of her hair several times before resigning herself to the windblown look.

Was Emma locked in a room without windows? In unfamiliar surroundings? She bowed her head over the railing, fighting back another round of nausea. Tears dampened her cheeks.

What if I fail her, if I can't solve my half of the puzzle? Maybe Nate's right. Maybe I'm not up to this and I'll slow him down until it's too late.

"Megan."

She glanced up to see the approaching dock. Swiping a hand across her eyes before weaving her way through the cars back to the Hummer, she determined to prove to Nate that she could handle this challenge. At least she could blame the tears on the ocean breeze.

Nate's place didn't surprise Megan at all. A three-story, boxy, modern-style house, it was tall and lean like its owner. The inside further reflected his military precision with minimalist furniture and décor, each item placed with an exactness that demonstrated his attention to detail. The dark, wood floors throughout brought just the right touch of comfort and masculinity to the room. Photos of him with Emma dotted the living room, splashes of warmth and color in an otherwise sterile environment.

Nate had left her in the living room, and when he reappeared he had a book of Sudoku puzzles in one hand and a Bible in the other.

"Mine has an inscription. Does yours?"

She opened the cover. "Yeah, John 12:3."

Nate set the Bible on the kitchen island and began thumbing through. "Mine's John 12:4-6." He stopped and ran a finger down the page, then read.

Then Mary took about a pint of pure nard, an expensive perfume; she poured it on Jesus' feet and wiped his feet with her hair. And the house was filled with the fragrance of the perfume.

But one of his disciples, Judas Iscariot, who was later to betray him, objected. "Why wasn't this perfume sold and the money given to the poor? It was worth a year's wages." He did not say this because he cared about the poor but because he was a thief; as keeper of the money bag, he used to help himself to what was put into it.

"What in the world does that mean?" Megan asked. "Better yet, how does it apply to our situation?"

"Break it down. An expensive perfume must mean Devastation. Dad said its value would be greater than Chanel No. 5."

Megan did some quick mental calculations, "Roughly six hundred dollars, so nowhere near a year's wages, although it's worth millions to the manufacturer. Where does that get us?"

"I doubt every part is relevant. It's the idea of the passage."

"Okay, it says Judas Iscariot was a thief and the keeper of the money bag. So the treasurer, right?"

Nate nodded in agreement.

"He also betrayed Jesus," Megan continued. "Is George saying that our treasurer is a thief and a traitor?"

"It's probably not that literal. But I'd say he's warning us about someone within the company."

"In other words, we need to keep this to ourselves." She wondered if she should confess her conversation with Sonia. Although she hadn't mentioned Emma's kidnapping...

"Hmmm," Nate replied.

Megan looked up to find him absorbed in his puzzle book. She swallowed her guilt and turned her concentration to her own puzzle. The long strings of jumbled letters without any hints were daunting. She guessed at one or two shorter words, coming up with botanical terms, but knew that without clues she'd never figure them all out. Her heart dropped.

"Latitude and longitude," Nate said with a note of triumph in his voice. "I was wondering how Sudoku was going to be a hint to anything, but in the center of the book there are several word puzzles on one page. If I take the solution to each one, I come up with a latitude and longitude."

"Maybe that's the key to my words. The couple I've been able to solve are plant names, although I can't imagine using them in a perfume. I must be missing something."

"So these are directions to the plants. The first one is on the island." He disappeared for a moment then returned with a map. Spreading it out, he did some calculations and drew a circle. "Here."

Megan came around to his side of the bar and peered at the map. "That's in the middle of state park land."

"Yep. We'll have to hike in." The look in Nate's eyes made it evident that he doubted her willingness or ability to do so.

Megan looked out the window. "It's already getting dark. We'll have to start tomorrow."

"Sunrise is at 0700 hours. We'll leave then. I'll pack a bag and stay over at Dad's tonight."

Megan refused to let him needle her. She fully intended to be up and ready for the hike at six a.m.

As Nate disappeared into his room to pack, Megan pulled out her cell phone. She had gotten a text from Sonia on the ferry but didn't want Nate to see her respond. He'd only get nosey.

did finance answer??

"No need," Megan responded.

worried about u. everything ok?

Of course Sonia could be trusted, but mindful of George's warning, Megan weighed her response.

"Busy. Will call tonight. Late. Okay?"

Plz. Dying to know what's happening.

Nate came back into the living room with his duffle bag packed. Megan stood by the counter fidgeting with her phone. Without a word exchanged between them, she followed him out to the Hummer, where he gave her a boost into the monstrous vehicle. Maybe it was time for a smaller truck.

The princess and the sailor? The probability was incalculable.

He cranked the engine and dismissed the idea before it took hold. Once Emma was home safe, they'd return to their designated roles. It was just the close proximity of the last twelve or so hours that had him off kilter. He glanced over at her as he waited for a light to change. Worry lined her face.

We'll find her, Megan. I promise to bring her home safe, if it's the last thing I do. The words contained too much emotion to say out loud. It could lead to an admission that he didn't want to return to their status quo.

He remembered her words as they boarded the ferry, and the truth of her argument was unsettling. His actions had accused her and Carol of stealing what was rightfully his, only he didn't want it. Couldn't put enough distance between himself and the perfume industry or Megan, for that matter. Crossing the bridge to the island, he made a decision. It was time to end the standoff and ask Megan for forgiveness.

He pulled into the driveway and turned off the ignition. Squirming in his seat, he tried to start the conversation.

"I, uh..." He cleared his throat. "There's something..."

Megan looked up at him, big blue pools dispelling all thoughts of apologizing. Fighting the draw of her eyes, he focused on her mouth, which reminded him of something else he had wanted to do for years.

"The note said there'd be a video." Her husky voice halted his thoughts.

"Right. 2200 hours. We'll use your laptop at the cottage." He pulled the keys out of the ignition.

"My military time's a little rusty." She released her seatbelt and turned toward him.

His feet hit the ground before he turned back to look at her, keeping his eyes schooled on a spot above her head. "Ten o'clock." He slammed the door on the incident. Without the ongoing hostilities, how would he defend his heart? He wasn't ready to surrender his defenses and risk an invasion.

Megan straightened the small dinette table in anticipation of Nate's arrival. What had he wanted to tell her? She'd never seen him display the slightest bit of uncertainty, but his discomfort tonight was obvious. If she didn't know better she'd think ... forget it. The thought was absurd. She opened her laptop and searched through her email until she found the link.

At ten p.m. on the dot, Nate knocked on her door.

Taking a deep breath, she opened it. "Hi. You're punctual." She stood in the doorway trying to gauge his mood. "I've got everything ready."

"Are you going to let me in?"

She backed up a little, and he strode past her to where she had her laptop set up on the table.

"Let's get this over with." He stood behind a chair.

The video. What message would it contain? Dread pushed her into the seat and she clicked the play button.

The camera stuttered, panned the floor, then jerked up to reveal brick walls in what looked like an old warehouse. The focus shifted to the right and Emma came into view. She sat on a metal folding chair, hands pulled behind her. Her long blonde hair was matted and mussed.

The scene transported Megan back to Friday night and the terror she had felt. Emma's dress was torn and filthy, her face tear-stained. A burlap hood hung around her neck and the mere sight of it had Megan struggling for air.

"Find the formula. I'll be safe if you find the formula." Emma choked out the words in a voice hoarse from crying.

Words scrolled across the bottom. *Same time tomorrow.* And then the screen went dark.

"0700. If you're late, I'll leave you here." Nate slammed the door behind him.

Chapter Five

Saturday, December 20, 11:00 p.m. – 63 hours remaining

Megan fisted her eyes in an effort to stop the flood. The video image remained on her computer screen with the play arrow obscuring Emma's face. But she couldn't X off the screen, couldn't close the computer lid—doing so would break all contact with Emma. Fresh tears welled up as she paced the kitchen floor. This treasure hunt thing was crazy. If they could just talk to George. She picked up her phone and tapped her mother's icon.

"Please answer, please answer."

"The mailbox is full," a robotic voice informed her.

"No, no. Where are you?" She scrolled down to George's number, but got the same response. How long had their phones been off that both mailboxes were full? And where had they gone if they weren't on their cruise?

She and Nate would have to follow the clues George had left in the puzzles. Unless there was another way to get her back. If law enforcement was forbidden, there must be someone else. A private investigator, a lawyer, *someone* they could contact.

You've watched too many movies. And to think she accused Nate of wanting to go all Hollywood hero. She snapped her fingers. She had promised Sonia she would call her tonight.

She slid her finger across the phone and then almost dropped it when it rang. Glancing at the screen, she smiled. *Great minds.*

"You won't believe this, but I was about to call you."

"I couldn't stand the suspense," Sonia said. "I hope you don't mind."

"You know I don't." She glanced at the frozen video image and drew in a ragged breath. "Emma's missing."

"What?" Incredulity filled Sonia's voice. "Missing like ... lost? Or run away?"

"Taken. She's been taken."

"Kidnapped? You've called the police, the FBI, right? Oh, poor George and Carol. I guess this has ruined their cruise. When will they get home?"

"They're not on their cruise. We don't know where they are."

"George and Carol are missing?"

"They're not answering their phones, and we haven't told anyone else. We can't tell anyone. I shouldn't be telling you. They'll kill her." Megan reached for a Kleenex as new tears threatened.

"That's why you were asking about emergency funds. I knew something was up. You can't hide from me, Megan. I know you too well. Look, I'll come home. I can be there in a few hours."

"Don't. They might find out. I shouldn't have told you, but I had to share it with someone who cares."

"No, you were right to tell me. I'll stay away if you think it's best for Emma ... whatever is best for her. Do you have any idea who would do this? What they want?"

"We're working on it. We'll figure it out." Megan dabbed at her eyes.

"Who's 'we'?"

"Nate. He's here, the... this person ... or persons, whoever they are, they contacted him."

"So you've heard their voice. Is it a man or a woman?"

"No. They sent letters. Crazy riddle letters and this awful video of her all beaten and dirty." Megan choked back a sob. "What are they going to do to her?"

"Oh honey, she's gonna be alright," Sonia said. "Listen, if you need some money..."

"They want some formula I've never heard of. Devastation."

"Oh, well that's easy. You know where George keeps the formulas."

"There wasn't a formula." Megan cried. "Just clues. Nate has half of them and I have the other half. We'll start looking in the morning."

"It must be pretty valuable if George went to all that trouble to secure it."

"I don't care what the formula's worth. I just want Emma back safe and sound." Megan turned her back on the computer screen.

"Of course you do," Sonia said.

"I'm wracking my brain trying to figure out who could be doing this."

Sonia put on her lawyer voice. "Let's think about this logically. If George developed a formula, he had to use the lab. Somebody may have seen him or helped him, realized the value of what he was working on. Does anyone come to mind?"

Megan performed a mental scan of the lab assistants and researchers. It had never occurred to her they may not be trustworthy. "I don't know. These are my co-workers, friends."

"Who else could know about a secret formula?"

Megan agreed it made sense to consider them, especially in light of George's letter. "Maybe ... no, it's not fair to judge."

"Your gut instinct is usually right."

"Well, it could be..." She hated to accuse someone without solid evidence, but these weren't normal circumstances. "Miles Bentley is kind of odd. But that doesn't mean he's a kidnapper."

"I know who you're talking about. Works in the lab at the end of the hall. A loner. Kinda creepy."

"Now Sonia, he's a bit awkward, that's all."

"Creepy."

"Okay, he's a little creepy." Megan walked to the kitchen door, checking that it was secure.

"You're his boss, check his personnel records. Google him."

"I don't want to invade his privacy."

"Megan, you're not playing a game. You're looking for a kidnapper. Emma's kidnapper. Do some digging!"

After the conversation ended, Sonia's suggestion haunted Megan. She ran her finger over the mouse and clicked on the internet browser. She logged in with her password and clicked through until she reached Miles Bentley's file, but she was unable to access it. A message box informed her that Miles had been George's special hire. His resume, background check, and references were sealed.

George often hired people other companies wouldn't touch. If George was convinced a person had truly turned from their past bad habits, whether it be substance abuse or criminal activity, he gave them a second chance. Had his generosity turned on him?

Megan Googled "Miles Bentley" in hopes of finding a clue to his history. Of the four listings in the US and the one in England, none of them were this Miles.

Sonia's assurances had calmed Megan down, but now she was too anxious to sleep. Could Miles Bentley hold the key to Emma's whereabouts? After a shower, she climbed into bed and reached for her Bible. Turning to Psalm 4, she started at the beginning.

"Answer me when I call to you, my righteous God. Give me relief from my distress; have mercy on me and hear my prayer."

I'm so glad you hear our prayers.

She read through to the last verse. "In peace I will lie down and sleep, for you alone, Lord, make me dwell in safety."

Lord, please give that peace and safety to Emma.

On the wings of her prayer, she found rest.

When the alarm buzzed, she stretched, thankful to wake from the nightmares. She hit the snooze and snuggled down under the covers. A moment later, her eyes popped open and her gaze landed on her dress, still lying on the floor. A sick feeling swallowed her as she threw back the covers and sat on the edge of the bed.

Nate woke from a restless sleep, took a quick shower, and proceeded down to the kitchen to prepare for the day. He had tried George's cell phone twice more last night, without success, leaving them with no other option than to chase clues. He stuffed two backpacks with supplies including frozen bottles of water and snacks. From his puzzle, he had mapped out their hike for the day. His weather app predicted a warm, sunny day with temperatures in the low 80s—typical winter weather in Florida. He pulled a pan from the overhead rack and broke a couple of eggs into a bowl.

"It'll be a hard day, but doable, if Megan doesn't wash out."

She's stronger than you give her credit for.

"Yeah, but will she be able to keep up on a grueling hike?" He whisked the eggs a little harder than necessary.

Give her a chance.

"I would, but this is too important. We can't afford to waste time." Nate threw some bacon strips into the hot pan and watched them sizzle. "Just keep Emma safe until I get there."

Because once you arrive I can take a break?

The sound of the back door opening should have ended the argument. But Nate was determined to get in the last word.

"Right on time, I'll give her that."

Nate's stony face greeted Megan when she walked into the kitchen of the main house.

She glanced at the wall clock. *Six-thirty and he's already angry at me.* "Good morning," she ventured.

He plunked a plate of eggs and bacon in front of her. The scent of it turned a stomach that had threatened to betray her all morning. "Not hungry." She pushed the food away and reached for the coffee pot.

"We won't be lunching at Antoine's." Nate pulled the barstool beside her and dug into his hearty breakfast.

Restless, Megan eased off the stool to wash dishes. Five minutes later, Nate set his plate in the water and picked up a pan to dry. As they worked together in silence, Megan recognized that some of the tension had left the air. Her mind drifted back to her research last night. "I've been thinking. The only people who could have known that George was working on a formula were those in the lab."

"That's a reasonable assumption, but they could have stolen it direct from the lab. There was no need to kidnap Emma." Nate hung the pan on the rack overhead.

"Except it was in his office safe."

"They tried to steal it and found the same thing we did—a puzzle requiring us to work together."

Megan drained the water from the sink and wiped down the countertops. "Did you know George sometimes hires people with...er, dubious backgrounds?"

He picked up a plate from the strainer. "He's mentioned that. He's also mentioned they're not treated any different from his other employees."

"Yeah, well, one of those hires was Miles Bentley."

"So?" Nate stacked a second dried plate on the first one and reached for the silverware.

"Well, if there's a crime, doesn't it make sense to look at people."

"The whole point of the program is that people not be judged by their past."

"I know, and I agree with that, except..." Megan stopped wiping the countertop and frowned at him. "Is it worth Emma's life?"

Nate handed her the towel. "So Miles Bentley is your suspect. What do you know about him?"

"Not much. I Googled him last night and couldn't find anything. Don't you think that's weird?"

Nate looked at the sky giving way to dawn. "I think we should stop speculating and hit the road."

By seven o'clock they were in the Hummer headed for the first location on Nate's map. He parked in a small clearing on the side of the two-lane road. Megan recognized the area. They were on a barrier island that was protected as a nature preserve. It had the barest amenities for human visitors. With some apprehension, she followed him down a narrow footpath until the dense cover of trees occluded the blue sky. Dew dampened the bottom of her jeans, and all around her unseen creatures moved, rustling the leaves. She couldn't help but search for the source amidst the thick underbrush.

"Careful," Nate said and ducked.

Megan skidded to a stop just short of the monstrous spider web that stretched across the trail. A large black and yellow spider stared at her from the middle. She caught her breath, imitated Nate and bent down to leave it undisturbed. As she continued down the path, she scrubbed her arms to get rid of the sensation of microscopic strings sticking to her.

An hour later, Megan was already feeling the effects of the hike—or rather jog, which was required to keep up with Nate's long stride. Fortunately, it was still somewhat cool in the woods. When they arrived at the first location, he turned and waited for her to catch up.

She reached the spot and studied the jumbled letters of her puzzle:

SORAVTAGLIEAA

Then she surveyed the plants. "Oh, look. There it is. A beautiful rosa laevigata."

"They all look the same to me." Nate snorted.

"No. This one is a Cherokee rose." She indicated the single thorny vine covered with delicate white flowers threaded through a wax myrtle bush. "The main plant must be through that thicket."

Nate headed into the woods.

"Don't go in there ... the thorns. I only need this one bloom." She plucked it from the vine and placed it in a plastic bag.

"Chasing after these stupid plants is a waste of time." Nate swatted branches out of his way.

"Don't you know what perfume is made of?"

"Never really thought about it." He rolled his eyes at her. "Trust me, when you're thirteen and in an all-boy's school, you wish your father did anything besides make perfume."

"It's chemistry. And he makes things other than perfume, like men's cologne, air fresheners, and fragrance for many daily products like soaps, shampoos, and lotions. Even cleaning products." Her argument was fruitless. Nate wasn't interested. "Oh, and surf wax."

"What?"

Ha. Knew that would appeal to the surfer.

"Last year, he came out with a surfboard wax. He insisted on the name NV Wax. The marketing department is having a field day with it." She knew George had named it for him, Nathan Vance, and she waited to see his reaction.

Nate's eyes widened and then he shook his head. "What's that smell like? Coconut or bubblegum?"

"Neither. It's a very clean scent with a hint of salt air."

They continued along the trail in silence for a while. Megan was too winded to talk. She hadn't done anything like this since that one semester of field study in college. Now she remembered why. The cute lace-up booties that had seemed a good choice last night blistered her heels. The soles were thin, and she could feel every acorn and twig underfoot.

At least the trail is easy to follow.

As if reading her thoughts, Nate pulled some branches aside. "We're taking it off-road."

As they slugged through the underbrush, branches pulled her hair out of its neat barrettes. A thorn bush halted her progress, ripping through her shirt and digging into the skin of her shoulder.

Nate turned back at her gasp and released her from the thorny grip. He inspected the wound with a cursory glance. "You'll live." Doing an about face, he continued down the nonexistent path.

As the descent became steeper, she leaned back to keep from tumbling forward down the hill. Wet leaves littered the floor of the woods, preventing the soles of her boots from gripping the slick surface. Her feet went flying and her arms flailed until she managed to clutch a branch and steady herself. Safe for the moment, she watched as Nate effortlessly bounded down ahead of her. She dug her feet into a firm stance and weaved her own way down with cautious steps.

At the bottom of the ravine, Nate stood waiting for her with his hands jammed into the pockets of his jeans. "Where did you get those ridiculous shoes?"

"Macy's." She noted his thick-soled leather boots. Deep ruts gave him solid traction. She opened her mouth to apologize for delaying him, but he turned his back and moved away. She followed, thankful they were at the bottom, until she was slogging through water up to her ankles. It sloshed into her boots and squished between her toes. She wrinkled her nose at the dank smell of the swamp and swatted at the gnats and no-see-ums that swarmed around her face. When she wanted to give up, she remembered Emma and how scared she must be. Silently she prayed for Emma and for herself to have the strength to make this trek.

As they rounded a bend sunlight burst through the trees, highlighting a bush of perky, yellow swamp sunflowers. Even Nate seemed to appreciate the beauty of their dancing heads.

While he examined his phone to confirm they were in the right location, Megan pulled out her plant book to verify the plant's scientific name. Helianthus angustifolius. She crossed out each of the jumbled letters as she placed them in their proper space. They fit. She blew out a breath. She had been worried about failure, but so far she was five for five. At each point Nate located on his map, Megan recognized a plant that matched a jumble on her puzzle.

A weight lifted off her shoulders. She had been trying so hard to please Nate, she hadn't realized that he needed her as much as she needed him, and that made them equal. She wasn't under the pressure of Nate's breakneck pace. Fidgeting with her phone, she took a few moments to catch her breath before standing up. She settled the heavy pack on her shoulders and turned to Nate. "Lead on."

An hour later, her newfound release had vaporized, melted by the sun bearing down on them. She still took time at each plant to regain her strength, but the short stops weren't giving her enough rest. She longed for a bottle of cold water like Nate kept sipping, but she wouldn't ask and invite his ridicule. The coolness of the ravine had been refreshing, but then they had to climb out of it. Unfortunately, that path was treeless. She thought Florida was flat, but she'd argue that point with anyone after today. Now it was all she could do to keep putting one foot in front of the other.

Nate stopped without warning, and Megan, who had long given up on admiring her surroundings, plowed into him.

"Pay attention or you'll walk into trouble," he said, steadying her. "We'll have lunch here." He indicated a semi-circle of cut logs that were set upright.

Megan glanced at her watch. Both hands approached twelve. She slid the backpack off her aching shoulders and perched her bottom on one of the hard logs. She didn't care. Her shins were screaming, and she didn't want to think about the blisters on her heels.

Nate sunk to the ground, using a log for a backrest, and munched on tuna and crackers he pulled from his backpack. Megan waited for him to share, as the half-slice of toast she had nibbled for breakfast was long gone. Fatigue had overwhelmed any nausea-inducing worries.

"Go ahead and eat." Nate pointed at her. "You're doing more than enough exercise to make up for a few crackers."

Ya think?

She hadn't packed a lunch. All she'd brought was a plant book and her phone that had an app for identifying the plants she took pictures of. She leaned forward, pretending to stretch her back, and fought the urge to cry. So she wasn't an outdoor girl. Her mom worked, and it fell to Megan to do the household chores. Camping, hiking, and fishing are things a girl does with her father. And he had left her. Packed his bags and walked out on her tenth birthday.

Wait a minute. Nate had given her the backpack, and it was really heavy. She picked it up and rummaged through it. Soon she came out with her own pack of tuna and crackers, along with a chilly bottle of water that had chunks of ice floating in it. Two more bottles wrapped in insulated covers were still frozen. She glanced at him in time to see him swallowing the last bite. Rising, he dusted himself off and tossed the remains in a trash can.

Please, let me stay long enough to eat.

He pointed to the path they were on. "I'm going to check the trail up ahead. I'll be back in five."

Relieved, she tore into the pack of tuna and scarfed it down. Now was not the time for decorum.

Giving Megan time to eat, Nate walked down the path and called his dad again. He got the same results—several rings followed by a click that ended the call. He shot a fist through the air. "Where are you, Dad?" It wasn't like him not to answer. Had something happened to them as well?

Frustrated, he strode through the woods and came to a bluff. Signs warned visitors to stay away from the edge. Below, uprooted trees and huge chunks of driftwood littered the beach. The waves lapping on shore took the edge off his anger and he began to calm.

He'd take his time, cool down, and give Megan a chance to rest. She had been a trouper. He could see the exhaustion in the slump of her shoulders, could hear the defeat in her robotic answers as she plodded behind him, barely able to put one foot in front of the other. Yet, she hadn't uttered one word of complaint all day. She was smart too. Not only did she hone in on the correct plant at each location, but she had found a way to rest at each stop.

She's tougher than she looks.

Wooden steps carried him down to Boneyard Beach, named for the massive trees scattered there. Gnarled roots and branches created an eerie, yet beautiful landscape of salt-washed skeletons that changed with the daily tides. Behind him, years of storms had eroded the soft sand, forming a large *C* and exposing the roots of trees that clung to the land above. Today, the inlet where river met ocean was deceptively calm. Picking up a stone, he skipped it across the water.

As the ripples spread, he considered Megan's comments at breakfast. Given her intelligence, maybe he should check out her hunch about Miles Bentley. She knew the employees of Harper Scents better than he did. He needed to update Paul on the status of the case, and it wouldn't hurt to let him check out the guy. He pulled his phone off his belt and made the call.

"We got the ransom demand," Nate said without preamble.

"How much?"

"It's not money. It's a formula, only we have to find the ingredients from a puzzle."

Spears let out a low whistle. "That's tough."

"It's ridiculous. I'm ready to mount a search-and-rescue effort."

"Careful cowboy. Industrial competition is fierce. These guys might be rougher than you think."

Nate picked up another stone and flung it across the water. "Since when is a perfume worth a little girl's life?"

"Never. That's why you've got to stay focused and get these guys what they want. For Emma's life."

"You're right. Hiking all over an island just seems counter-productive."

"How did the ransom demand come?" Spears asked.

"Another cryptic letter, delivered the same as the others."

"Any suspects?"

Nate had spent the night mulling over that question and had come to the same conclusion as Megan, only he hadn't had the name. "Possibly research and development. Check out a guy named Miles Bentley."

"I'm on it."

"Great. Thanks." Nate started to hang up but remembered something. "Hey, Spears. Can you trace an IP address?"

"Sure. You got an email from them?"

"Yeah, proof-of-life video. She's a little battered and bruised, but overall she's healthy."

"That's a relief." Paul repeated the IP address Nate gave him. "You know this is a long shot—that it could have been bounced through several servers or sent from a public network."

"It's the only shot I've got."

He hung up feeling better for the talk with Paul. Between Megan's knowledge of the Harper Scent employees and Paul's investigative instincts, they might have their first real lead. If Miles Bentley had any dirty laundry, Paul would find it. And if the IP address was traceable, Paul would uncover that, too.

His mind drifted back to Megan. It was time to admit he had been wrong about her. He kicked himself for the way he had treated her. His bungled attempt to apologize last night made him feel like the awkward teenager he had worked so hard to distance himself from. Determined to keep his emotions under control, he had entered the cottage with a no-nonsense attitude. The video drove that out of him, replacing it with anger at those who had taken Emma and a desire to shield Megan from those images. He'd expected Megan to fall apart, a scene he wouldn't have been able to bear. But she showed remarkable restraint, although silent tears coursed down her cheeks. He could tell it took every ounce of her willpower to hold it together. She needed his strength and comfort, but he was too busy protecting himself. He'd uttered harsh ultimatums and left her alone with her fear.

Lord, please forgive me.

Again, the Spirit convicted him. He needed to ask for her forgiveness. He wasn't sure how, but he could start by not compounding the error. With a new resolution to treat Megan with kindness and respect, Nate headed back to the picnic area. He found her curled up on the ground, fast asleep.

A fifteen-minute power nap won't hurt.

Watching the steady rise and fall of her breathing, the sensation snuck up on him. It wasn't a noise or a smell, but that sixth sense developed in combat that warns of the enemy's presence. He surveyed the dense forest in front of him and saw nothing. Stretching, he rose to his feet and searched the woods behind him without result. Still the feeling remained.

As much as Megan deserved sleep, they had several hours of hiking ahead and dark would be upon them soon. He knelt beside her.

"Megan."

Her eyes opened, and he thought he saw a flash of welcome before confusion and anxiety crashed in.

"I must have ... I'm so sorry." She jumped to her feet.

"It's okay. You're identifying the plants so fast that we can slow down some this afternoon." He settled the backpack onto her shoulders.

They continued their hike with the river to their left. Their footsteps disturbed woodland creatures who scurried into hiding, but he heard no human sounds. Blaming an overactive imagination, he dismissed the sense of foreboding.

When they rounded a bend and stopped at the next mapped location, Megan knelt before a bush. The birds hushed their singing, and an eerie silence descended. He searched again for the threat, finding none. As the path led them away from the river and back to the ocean side of the island, the hairs on the back of his neck laid down. Maybe they had crossed paths with a photographer or naturalist.

Nate reached the crest of the sand dune and mopped his forehead. The sun beat down as the temperature climbed into the mid-80s. He glanced at his watch—almost two o'clock, the hottest part of the day. Rivulets of sweat glided down his spine as he reached the top of the narrow trail lined with thickets of palmetto bushes on each side. He turned to watch Megan as she struggled up the sand dune with mulish tenacity, the sand pulling her down a step for every two steps up. The nap had done her a world of good, but it was clear her energy was flagging. He pulled his phone out of his pocket to check the next coordinates. Megan reached the plateau beside him and bent over, hands on knees, to catch her breath.

"You can take the lead for a while," he said.

She nodded and set off down the dune, and he trailed behind. A few paces later, she stumbled. He reached for her and missed. As she fell headlong into the sand, he heard the distinct rattle. The coiled form lay inches from Megan's leg.

"Don't move."

Chapter Six

Megan heard a strange buzzing noise and froze. Nate's order confirmed her fear. She wanted to know what he was doing, but she was facing away from him.

"Stay calm," Nate said, but from a greater distance this time.

"Where are you going? Don't leave me."

The buzzing started again, like a swarm of bees. Every muscle in her body tightened in expectation of being bit at any moment. Megan fought the urge to jump up and run.

"I'm giving him space. He'll move on."

Megan wasn't so sure.

"Keep still. He's moving away from you."

She squeezed her eyes shut and bit her upper lip for what seemed an eternity.

And then Nate was crouched beside her with a gentle hand on her arm. "You're safe now."

She clasped his outstretched hand and scrambled to her feet. Looking back up the dune, she saw the telltale *S* track in the sand. A shudder went through her.

"Snakes are our friends," Nate said with a straight face.

Did he actually make a joke? Megan gave him a scorching look.

He chuckled and took the lead down the path.

They came out of the dunes onto the firmer, wet sand of the beach as a strong breeze blew in from the ocean, cooling them off. Nate stopped at the next location.

"Sea oats, that's all I see." Megan scrutinized the area for some small, insignificant flower or plant she was missing. She pulled the puzzle out of her pocket and looked at the jumbled letters.

E M O P A I O E S R P A C E P A

Uniola paniculata, the scientific name for sea oats, wasn't coming out of those jumbled letters. She looked at the dune closer, and then she spotted it. "There." She pointed to a small leaf. "Railroad vine, or Ipomoea pes-caprae."

Nate followed her pointing finger. "There's no railroad around here."

"It doesn't sound very beachy, but it often twines itself along the floor of the dunes, hiding under the sea oats and creating a natural protection against erosion." She filled in blanks and crossed out jumbled letters. "And it fits." She smiled triumphantly. "Where to next?"

Nate studied his phone screen. "I think that's it for today. The next coordinates take us over to Dolphin Island. We'll need a kayak."

"So what's the problem? Let's get started."

Nate glanced at his watch. "It's too late in the day. It's going to take us an hour to get back to the Hummer, then back home, load the kayak, and drive to the launching spot. We'd get caught by dark."

"We'll just have to push through it. Emma is depending on us."

"But you can't identify plants in the dark, so what good would it do?" He walked away from her. "We'll start fresh tomorrow."

In her mind she knew he was right, and her body was beyond ready to call it a day. But her heart told her every minute counted. She wondered what Emma was going through right now while they walked carefree along the beach. A chill ran up Megan's spine as she imagined Emma in a dark, rat-infested chamber with no one to comfort her. A more horrifying image of her being beaten or otherwise abused sent Megan into a fury. She ran to catch up with his easy strides and jumped in front of him to block his progress.

"How can you be so callous? First you refuse to report her missing to the cops. Okay, I get that they might be watching us. But now you want to take an eight-to-five approach to solving this? You must not care as much about Emma as you claim, or you'd be moving heaven and earth to find her!"

Nate stared at her as if she had lost her mind before he blinked and walked around her without a word. His indifference sent her temper soaring. She grabbed at his arm in an attempt to turn him around and her nails sliced into his skin, leaving a bloody trail.

A thundercloud descended on his features as he looked first at his arm and then at her.

She covered her mouth with her hand. "I ... I'm sorry."

Nate strode away, leaving her to stare at his back. What had possessed her to say such cruel words? She knew he cared for Emma every bit as much as she did. And, although the day had started out a little rocky, he'd been quite considerate of her all afternoon. So why had she broken the mood?

She trudged down the beach behind him, kicking herself for allowing her frustration and tiredness to get the better of her.

As Nate parked the Hummer under the portico to the main house, Megan forced herself into a state of wakefulness. Lifting her backpack from the floorboard, she reached for the door as he pulled it open. Exhausted, she accepted his proffered hand and slid from the seat to the ground. She studied his face for residual signs of anger, but his expression remained an enigma.

"I'll be at the cottage at ten." Nate released her hand.

She nodded, thankful she had a few hours to indulge her weariness. She entered the cottage and tossed her backpack on the bed, then hobbled into the bathroom. She spun the faucet to fill the tub with hot water. As the steam formed a fog around her, she closed her eyes and basked in the warmth.

Keeping up with Nate all day had drained her physical strength, leaving her legs and back aching from the unusual exercise. But it had distracted her from Emma's plight. Now, images of Emma shivering on a metal cot invaded her mind. There were so many kidnappings in the news and, although some victims like Elizabeth and Jaycee escaped, the horrific details of their ordeal assailed her. How many others were still captives? What was Emma suffering? Megan's throat burned as tears rolled down her face unchecked.

Lord, please keep her safe. Help us to find her soon.

It was still several hours before the video. If she sat here with her thoughts she'd go mad. Drying off, she dressed in a hurry and reached for her phone. Sonia was the only person who knew and could sympathize with her situation. Talking to her friend might be helpful. After all, Sonia had got her thinking of Miles Bentley as a suspect. Maybe they could brainstorm some more ideas.

Sonia's mix of concern and humor was the balm Megan needed as she related the day's events.

"A rattlesnake? You're lucky Nate was with you."

"You know, he was kinda nice this afternoon." Megan placed a pre-cooked meal in the microwave and set the timer.

"The way you described him—cold, imposing—I expected an ogre. But he's good-looking in those pictures George has. And then when I saw him at the Fourth of July picnic—wow."

"Yeah, I was pretty awestruck the first time I met him, but I was just seventeen. It didn't take long for his personality to kill the infatuation."

"The problem is you're attracted to each other."

"You're crazy." Megan pulled the plate out of the microwave, dropped it on the counter and blew at her fingers.

"Nope, I'm serious. You two are magnets, always repelling the other. You just need to flip your attitude, drop your guard. Trust me. I know men, and Nate is magnetized."

Megan swallowed a bite. "I'm not the one who needs to flip. I get him not being happy when our parents first married. I wasn't too thrilled with the situation either, but at least I tried to be pleasant. He's gone from chilly to downright frigid." Although, she had noted a warming trend with possible thawing. And this afternoon, one chunk of ice had melted. But would it last? The danger with ice was frostbite.

"I'll be happy to share my theory with him." Sonia laughed.

"Yeah, I don't think so. Speaking of the Fourth of July..."

"Changing the subject?"

"Yes, I am." Megan rose from the table to fill her glass. "Remember Nate's friend? Wasn't he some kind of private investigator?"

"I don't know. I was feasting my eyes on Nate, who, by the way, didn't acknowledge my existence." Sonia teased.

"That's not true. He teamed up with you in volleyball."

"Only as a favor to you."

"C'mon Sonia, the private investigator. He's not law enforcement, not technically. He could help us find Emma. It was a Bible name ... what was it?"

"Mark, John, Luke, Matthew?" Sonia offered.

"No, it was Peter or, or Paul. That's it. Paul. I wonder how I can get in touch with him."

"If you want this PI's help, you'd better go through Nate. Listen honey, I really think the best thing is to follow the clues. I know it's frustrating, but it's what the kidnappers want. Bringing in someone else is taking a huge risk."

Megan swallowed a bite and chased it down with a drink of water. "I'm glad I told you."

"Me too, but I'm harmless moral support. A private investigator is going to dig around, make them nervous—and that could be bad for Emma."

"You're right, you're right. I just..."

"I get it. You want to be proactive, to get her out of danger right now."

A knock on the door prevented Megan's answer. "Nate's here. It's time to watch the second video."

"Okay, but remember ... magnets."

Megan pressed the end button and stowed her half-eaten supper in the fridge before opening the door. She didn't block his entrance tonight. After he brushed past her, he turned and laid a hand on her shoulder.

"I'm not looking forward to this any more than you are, but every night they send a video we at least know she's alive."

His words were oddly comforting as she settled into a chair and turned on the computer. The cameraman did a better job this time. The video focused on Emma, still in her dirty dress, bruised like before. The current date flashed in the corner.

"Nate, Megan, please come get me." Emma's trembling voice sent a shudder through her.

The screen went dark before Emma finished saying the last word. Megan ran her finger across the screen. "Emma, I'm so sorry I let you down."

She turned to Nate. "It's my fault we didn't make it to Dolphin Island today. If I hadn't slowed you down, you could have made better time."

Nate squatted in front of her. "But I couldn't have identified the plants."

His change in attitude perplexed her. She expected him to seize the opportunity to be rid of her. "You can take my phone tomorrow. Take a picture and the app will identify it."

"I don't know what to take pictures of. I didn't even see that rose thing this morning." Reaching out, he tucked a loose strand of hair behind her ear.

His hand lingered on her cheek, infusing her with warmth. She closed her eyes and leaned into his gentle strength.

"It won't be so hard tomorrow. We'll be in a kayak." He stood and walked out of the cottage.

Megan stared at the door Nate had closed behind him. In all their past encounters, he had treated her with disdain. His kindness threw her off balance. Perhaps he wanted the formula so he could seize control of Harper Scents. She dismissed the idea at once. He had never shown any interest in the company, so it didn't make sense that he would go to such lengths now. More likely, he was afraid she'd fall apart and he did need her help. Whatever the reason for his change, she was grateful.

She began laying out her clothes for tomorrow. She wasn't going to burn up again, so she pulled out some lightweight Capri pants and a tank top with a cotton over-shirt for the cool morning. A cursory examination had confirmed the blisters on her heels, so the hiking boots were out. She found an old pair of flip flops that were sturdy enough for walking. Restless, she strolled over to the window and pulled the curtains aside. The full moon had risen, illuminating a narrow section of the ocean like a spotlight. She dropped the curtain and crawled into bed, but sleep evaded her.

Chapter Seven

Monday, December 22, 2:00 a.m. - 36 hours remaining

The video angered him. Nate hadn't felt so helpless since his teenage years. He had vowed then never to be at the mercy of someone bigger than himself. And yet, here he was fighting an unknown enemy, forced to jump through ridiculous hoops in the hopes of saving his sister. He longed to get his hands on the animal that had bound a young girl and coerced her to beg for her life.

When they had gathered all the clues for the formula, he would counterstrike. He would neutralize the traitor and rescue Emma. Jogging from the cottage to the main house, he plotted the operation, envisioning the revenge he would exact.

Focus on the current mission.

Nate entered the study of the main house and began organizing his intel. The coordinates took them to a remote saltwater marsh island in the intra-coastal waterway. He clicked on his weather app and frowned. A small craft advisory and a nor'easter. He calculated the time it would take to reach the island and return. Difficult conditions would slow their progress, but if they started early enough they had a chance to beat the storm.

Delay wasn't an option. They were already down to less than forty-eight hours to solve the puzzle, and Emma's life depended on them sticking to the schedule. Although he considered Megan's offer to lend him her phone with the plant app, he discarded the idea as too risky. Missing an important ingredient could jeopardize the outcome. Megan was the plant expert and vital to the mission. He'd escorted experts on dives before. Escorting her would be no different.

He gripped the desk, fighting the specter that pierced his brain. He'd protect her with his life. It was his absolution.

This time I'll get it right.

Determined to atone his past, he studied the maps, looking for the most protected path. But there was only one course in and out. At least they wouldn't be in direct contact with the ocean, although the wind and swells pushing eastward would make the Amelia River treacherous. He spent another hour in preparation. Confident he had everything ready for the mission, he climbed into bed.

Lying flat on his back, he continued to review his options. He had to be absolutely sure that he and Megan made it safely to the island and back. He ran through every possible obstacle and how he would overcome it. Tension seized him in its relentless grip. He realized sleep would elude him until he shut off his mind, so he left the house and strolled down to the beach.

Dark clouds scuttled across the sky as Nate waded into the ocean. Going farther out, he battled through the rough surf worsened by the approaching storm. He dove into an oncoming wave and swam parallel to the shore. He reached his normal turning point expecting to be exhausted, but his muscles remained tense. He treaded water a few minutes, testing his energy level. Since his mind continued to race, he dove deep and propelled himself back the way he had come, testing the limits of his lungs until they burned from lack of oxygen. Then he punished them a little longer. Seconds before blacking out, he burst through the surface of the water. He filled his lungs with air and dove again. He emerged once more, checked his stop watch, and was pleased with his underwater time. Constant training kept him prepared for any situation.

Readiness. That's what he drilled into the men he trained. No man left behind. Watch your buddy's back. But at the end of the day, he was the one responsible for everyone on the team. He had failed that test once. He didn't dare fail it again ... not with Emma's life at stake.

Not by force, nor by strength, but by my Spirit.

He reached his starting point and trudged out of the water, his body beyond exhausted, though his mind remained disquieted.

He still felt guilty for being so hard on Megan earlier in the day. The short cut through the swamp had been unnecessary. They could have stayed on the path and gotten there without soggy feet, even though it would have taken a little longer. But no matter how hard he pushed her, she kept up. He knew she was struggling, but she didn't let on. He admired that in new recruits. He'd keep driving his men to build character and strength. But she wasn't one of his trainees, so he'd let up on her, especially after lunch, and more so after she kept her cool during the rattlesnake incident. She proved she was a team player by relying on him when she couldn't see what the creature was doing behind her. Her courage amazed him.

You judged her on appearance, the same preconceptions you suffered.

Okay, so he'd learned his lesson.

You still haven't apologized to her. Haven't asked for her forgiveness.

His change in attitude *was* his apology. Besides, she's the one who broke the truce with her ludicrous allegations. He brushed his arm in memory. The accusations and scratches were nothing compared to the pain caused by the gut-wrenching anguish in her eyes. That's why he had turned his back on her. Her suffering left him undone. Diplomacy was one thing, surrender was another.

He stopped in his tracks and searched the beach as the hair on the back of his neck stood on end. When he looked up toward the bluff where the house overlooked the water, he saw Emma, bathed in moonlight, the wind pushing her blonde hair from her face. She was so tiny, if her hair were a sail, she would fly away. Then the figure turned and fled. He ran up the beach to catch her. Emma couldn't have been right here all along. They wouldn't have released her before they obtained the formula. Had she escaped?

When he reached the grassy knoll, the lawn was vacant. He ran to the pool area of the main house, searching in the shadows. The wind howled, but during a break he heard a soft whimper and found her crouched in the corner between the outdoor fireplace and the stone wall of the house. He knelt down in front of her.

"It's okay, kiddo. I'm here. You're safe."

She flung herself into his arms, almost knocking him off balance. "I can't sleep. I hear them, smell them," she sobbed. "I thought you were one of them. I was so afraid they were coming back to get me too."

It took him a full minute to realize it wasn't Emma in his arms. Disappointment, anger, and tenderness fought for first place in a tornado of emotions. He coaxed her out of the shadows and stared down at her as he brushed wind-teased hair away from her face then cupped his hands around it. The moon escaped its cloud cover, confirming his suspicions.

Megan.

She chewed on her lower lip, her eyes darting side to side. She looked ready to bolt, so Nate drew her into his arms. He felt her relax as she laid her head on his chest and wrapped her arms around his waist. He stroked her back while his mind changed gears.

She fit so right in his arms he didn't want to let go—ever. If he continued to comfort her, he'd give in to his attraction. It was time to apologize for his past actions, regain control.

"Megan," he whispered as his lips moved across the top of her hair.

She lifted her head, gazing at him with an intensity that invaded his soul. He mounted the only defense he knew—distance.

Megan's feet left the ground as Nate propelled her backward with a steel grip on her elbows. He set her down in a lounge chair, turned his back, and strode to the edge of the patio. Clearly he couldn't get away from her fast enough.

She covered her face, mortified at her behavior.

He whirled to face her, arms crossed over his chest. "Couldn't sleep, huh?"

She nodded, shivering at the sudden coolness, bereft of his warm embrace. He stared, appraising her, and she fought the urge to squirm like a child in the principal's office.

"The weather's deteriorating."

Her mouth dropped open. *Really? You're going to discuss the weather?*

"There's a full moon. If we leave now, we can make Dolphin Island by first light, whatever light there's going to be."

Not understanding his weather talk, but not wanting to anger him, Megan agreed. She dashed to the cottage to prepare for their trip, still befuddled by the sudden change in Nate's attitude.

As she entered her room, the bedside lamp she'd left on bathed it in warmth and quieted her nerves. Despite his personal disdain for her, Megan knew Nate to be a kind and considerate person. She had seen it in his relationships with others, more so in the last year since he had been stationed at nearby Mayport. She alone possessed the particular gift of raising his ire. And it had nothing to do with magnets, no matter what Sonia said.

She pulled on the clothes she had laid out earlier, finishing off with a sweater. With a quick survey in the mirror, she squared her shoulders to face another strenuous day.

Nate busied himself cooking a hearty breakfast in an attempt to keep his mind off Megan. Angry with himself for being unable to focus on the task at hand, he grabbed a single backpack—no need to burden her with the additional weight—and stuffed it with thermoses of coffee and bags of snacks. The apology wasn't happening. He had made two bungled attempts, resulting in more harm than good. The only solution was to leave. As soon as they finished this insane treasure hunt and could rescue Emma, he'd put in for a transfer. Alaska might be far enough away.

Megan walked in the door, proving his strategy easier planned than executed. Her hair was tussled by the wind, and dark circles shadowed her blue eyes, emphasizing the paleness of her skin. She appeared tired and fragile, tearing him up inside. Why couldn't he just tell her she was a valuable asset to be safeguarded? That would charm her socks off. He'd worked so hard at maintaining a distance with people that he found it difficult to switch gears. One more obstacle to conquer.

"Shouldn't you wear something warmer?" He evaluated her short pants and flip flops.

"I'm good." She wrapped the thick, oversized sweater tighter around her middle, like a child clinging to a blanket.

"There's a nor'easter brewing." He moved toward her, searching for the right words.

She stared him back.

Fine.

They ate in tense, uncomfortable silence. Everything he wanted to say sounded too stilted in his head. The food became chalk in his mouth. When he had choked down an adequate amount, he washed it away with a gulp of coffee and put the dishes in the sink.

Megan rose to his silent signal. He held a rain slicker as she slid her arms into it, careful not to touch her. Hoisting the backpack on his shoulder, he opened the door to the portico for her to pass through. The family had every type of sporting equipment imaginable, and he had loaded a double kayak from the garage onto the Hummer last night. Once they were in the vehicle, he broke the silence.

"Ever kayak?"

"A few times in college. I won't hold you back."

There it was again—her chin jutted out in a manner that said she wouldn't let him see her sweat. He couldn't fault her defiance after all the times he had thrown insulting terms at her.

He blew out a long breath. Tired of the war between them, he longed for a ceasefire. But her defensiveness made that impossible. Maybe it was for the best. A break in his well-constructed dike would allow a flood of emotion that would wash away the wall in its entirety. For the time being, he'd have to continue to be the tough guy and hide his feelings. Fortunately, he had a lifetime of experience in that field.

As he pulled into the boat launch parking lot, clouds blanketed the sky and the moon produced only a faint glow through them. He and Megan worked in the reduced light to get the kayak into the water.

While Megan slid into place, Nate placed his gear—map, coordinates, compass, and phone—in a clear, dry case then looped the lanyard around his neck and under his rain slicker. No sooner had they pushed away from the dock than the drizzle began, light at first and then increasing to a steady rain.

Megan shivered under the rain slicker, thankful Nate had provided it. At least he was semi-concerned about her health.

Probably doesn't want to be bothered with taking me to the hospital.

She dug her paddle in the water and pushed against the current with all her might. Nate had informed her with his usual brusqueness that Dolphin Island was ten miles away and then waited for her to balk. She wasn't sure what she was in for, but she would make it. *For Emma.* Showing Nate that she wasn't the debutante he accused her of being was icing on the cake.

Her bravado crumbled in the face of reality. Knots formed in her shoulders and neck. Her arms burned as she lifted the paddles that transformed to lead with every stroke. The muscles in her outstretched legs screamed for freedom. Wiggling, she tried to find a comfortable position for her back. It seemed like hours since they had started out, although it was difficult to tell with the clouds hanging so low. A gray and swirling mist shrouded them, blending the water and sky into one. She trusted Nate to navigate through the darkness to their destination, but what if they were lost, rowing in circles?

To her left she saw the shore and sighed with relief.

Nate shouted to be heard over the wind. "That's Little Dolphin. We've still got a mile to go."

Gritting her teeth against the pain, she responded in her most cheerful voice. "Great. I'm just hitting my stride."

Twenty minutes later, Nate vaulted out of the kayak into shallow water. He studied his phone in its waterproof case while Megan struggled to wiggle out of her prison.

The beach was little more than a sandbar surrounded by a grassy plain flooded with sea water and filled with creatures she had no desire to encounter. Palm trees missing their heads and ancient cypress trees with their sparse branches reached high into the gray mist. In the distance, a small forest indicated higher ground.

"We'll hike inland a mile or so." Nate started up the trail.

Megan took off after him and promptly sunk up to her ankles in the mud of the salt marsh. Fighting the suction, she pulled her feet out minus a shoe. By the time she dug it out, Nate was retracing his steps. Great, she was already slowing him down.

"I'm fine." She stomped to prove she had a firm footing. He turned with a shrug and she raced to catch up with his long strides.

The rain had stopped, but moisture filled the air. Megan shuddered as the damp fingers of cold wrapped around her exposed legs.

They reached a wooded hammock where massive oak trees provided shelter from the elements. Leaves covered the dirt floor, and the path became much easier to walk.

Nate stopped at the first coordinate and waited for her to catch up. "Use your magic eyes."

They followed the same routine as yesterday, working in silence. The tension seemed to be easing between them. Maybe it was wishful thinking, but she tried to focus on the positives. It felt good to stretch her legs and rest her arms. Of greater importance, they were closer to obtaining all the ingredients that would ransom Emma. When she had identified all five plants, Nate added the samples and her puzzle book to his backpack.

"Let's take a break before we head back," he said as he pulled a thermos and energy bars from his sack.

"Thanks." Megan accepted the food and drink he offered. She hadn't realized how hungry she was.

"Now that we have all the ingredients, do you think this formula is valuable?" Nate took a swig of coffee.

"To be honest, no." Megan frowned. "Some of the plant choices yesterday seemed peculiar, but these today make absolutely no sense. They're not even aromatic."

"Why would Dad create a formula that's worthless?"

"I don't know, unless it's more about the hunt or solving the puzzle within the puzzle." She leaned against a tree and munched her snack.

"Here's a clean, dry area where we can sit."

"I'll stand." She regretted her tone when he narrowed his eyes at her. "Sorry. I'm just tired and tight from sitting in the kayak all morning. I'd rather stand for now."

"Suit yourself." He dropped to the ground, pulled out his phone, tapped the screen, and proceeded to ignore her.

As Megan stood still, it felt as though the temperature dropped. She waited on Nate while her bare legs and feet grew colder. Pulling her arms out of the poncho, she drew the thick sweater tight around her, except it was damp from the earlier rain and did nothing to warm her. When Nate put away his phone and rose, she was glad to be on the move again.

Once they left the protection of the hammock, the gray skies leaked a drenching mist and wind whipped across the low marsh grasses with icy pellets. Megan's limbs were numb from the cold and the rest of her wasn't much warmer. No amount of clothing seemed to stop the air from penetrating each layer she wore. As they climbed into the kayak, the rain renewed its strength. They now paddled through a deluge of gray sheets.

Any hope of the hull providing warmth and protection evaporated as frigid rain drops dripped off the paddles and slithered their way to Megan's legs. The wind blew the rain sideways, stinging her face like pieces of glass. Nate's broad back prevented her from seeing anything had she been inclined to look, but it did little to protect her from the sideways attack. She bowed her head against the onslaught and paddled with dogged determination.

Emma, Emma, Emma. She chanted to herself with each stroke.

Nothing she went through yesterday or would go through today was as horrible as what Emma was suffering. She moved into a zone of robotic rhythm, beyond pain, operating on sheer willpower and determination. It took a few minutes for Nate's voice to penetrate her intense focus. He was yelling over the wind, but the words were incomprehensible.

Lifting her head, she saw a wall of water above them. She took a deep breath and then the weight of the wave was crushing her. Spinning and spiraling, she opened her eyes, unaware she had closed them. Bubbles and foam rose around her, and something wrapped around her head, blocking her view. Clawing at the slimy seaweed, she freed it from her eyes and looked at the compartment in front of her. No Nate. She kicked with her feet, but the kayak held her in its unyielding grip, trapped underwater.

Chapter Eight

Monday, December 22, 2:00 p.m. – 24 hours remaining

Nate grappled with the ghosts from his past. Images of Taylor and Johnson so real he reached out to grab them.

I've got to save them. Got to save them.

He wrangled himself free from the kayak and burst through the surface of the water. The slap of a cold wave woke him to his current reality.

Megan.

He scanned the water, looking for any sign of her. Diving under, he found her, feet caught in the overturned kayak, eyes closed. She swayed to and fro in the current. Terror seized him. What if he couldn't save her? After all, he had been unable to save his buddies. And he hadn't attempted an ocean rescue since that fateful day. He worked to free her while the memory crowded his mind.

Taylor's eyes had widened as he realized his breathing apparatus had failed. Johnson had approached him to assist, but Taylor's flailing arms had prevented it. Then, in a moment of panic, Taylor had ripped off Johnson's mask. As a result, they both needed rescuing, and Nate could only save one of them, forced to choose between teammates. Holding the gift of life for one meant withholding it from the other. In the end, he hadn't been able to save either of them.

Fear's cruel hand held Nate in its grip as he struggled to pull Megan's legs free from the kayak. Stubborn pride had kept him from exploring his feelings for her, and now he was in danger of losing her. Even if she survived, he may have procrastinated too long, rebuffed her too often. And if he couldn't save Megan who was right here, he didn't have a chance of saving Emma. He didn't even know where she was. Without Megan, he had no hope of finding her.

Not acceptable.

He utilized the adrenaline to pull Megan's limp body from the kayak and fight to the surface.

As Megan's head broke the surface, she drew in a deep breath, which sent her into a coughing spasm. Nate held her up until she was able to catch her breath.

"You okay?"

Megan nodded, still gulping air.

"Hold onto the kayak. Don't leave it under any circumstances."

"Where are you going?" She brushed wet strands of hair out of her eyes with her free hand.

Nate grabbed her arm and put her hand back on the vessel. "Both hands on the 'yak. Got it?"

She shrunk from his harshness. He had never manhandled her before. "Right." She hugged the hull with both arms.

He fixed on her with a long stare. Then he disappeared.

She looked around. Water everywhere, waves crashing around her and over her. The boat bobbed, its slick hull making it difficult to cling to. Something wrapped around her feet, and she kicked in a frenzied effort to free herself.

Where was Nate?

It seemed too long for him to have been under water without air. Dreadful scenarios bombarded her mind. He could be injured or trapped. Perhaps she should ignore his command and leave the boat to find him.

A wave washed over her, leaving her sputtering and spitting. She hauled herself higher up on the kayak, almost submerging it in the process.

Maybe he had swum away, leaving her to fend for herself. He had all the ingredients for the formula now. What was to prevent him from running with it? No one would miss her for days, and if they did, no one had any idea where she was. No other boaters would be out on a day like this. If she didn't try to swim for shore, she would die.

Stop it!

Rain poured from the sky, blocking any sign of land. The cold was numbing and she slipped off the hull. She clawed down the smooth sides, desperate to find a hand hold. Pushing aside the negative thoughts, she looked for some levity.

I could use an ark about now.

She summoned her natural optimism. Nate was an expert in water rescue. He had rescued her from the kidnappers and nursed her back to health. He discovered the coordinates for the puzzle, kept her from being snake bitten, and had saved her from drowning just now. At times, he had even been considerate and compassionate. So for all his arrogance and sarcasm, she had full confidence in his ability to bring them out of this mess unharmed— and ultimately to bring Emma home.

After what seemed an eternity, Nate's head popped out of the water and he held up the backpack containing the plant samples and all their supplies. He shook his head to remove the excess water, but rivulets still ran down his face. "What kind of a swimmer are you?"

Megan's heart sank. "Can't we just flip over the boat?"

Nate shook his head. "It's not far. If you get tired, I'll carry you." He pointed out the direction. "You start. I'll catch up."

True to his word, Nate stayed by her side or a little ahead. He'd switch to a back stroke to keep an eye on her. He constantly monitored her progress and gave her encouragement. This was not the brusque Nate she knew. She was buoyant under his praise. Eager to earn his respect, she pushed through the formidable waves. The tide worked against them, and she earned each rigorous yard. After a time, her heavy sweater that had been so comforting became cumbersome and her arms, already fatigued from rowing, gave way. She drifted farther away from Nate, who was swimming ahead at the moment. She tried to call out, but her feeble voice couldn't compete with the wind and waves. She closed her eyes and floated face down.

Rest, just a minute to rest.

Then Nate was by her side, lifting her head out of the water and removing the bulky sweater. "C'mon Meg. Don't give up on me now." He held her chin in his hand.

She tried to focus on his blurring image. "Too tired," she murmured, closing her eyes. "You go."

"Relax. I've got you."

He held her up as he swam toward safety. Trusting in his ability, she drifted in the security of his arm around her.

When Nate stood in the shallow water, Megan tried to follow his lead, but her legs folded beneath her. Salt water burned through her nostrils and down her throat. She tried to stand again and failed, so Nate scooped her up in steel-banded arms. Once out of the water, her sodden clothes turned to icy rags as the sharp wind whipped around her. She shivered uncontrollably, and her teeth chattered.

His lips brushed her hair and he whispered, "I'm sorry, honey. We're almost there."

She couldn't have heard right. Must be an exhaustion-induced hallucination. Still, she tightened her arms around his neck and buried her face in his chest.

When they reached the Hummer, Nate eased her into the seat. He drew a lingering hand down her face, cradling it for a moment. Her eyes locked with the soft gray of his and the cold vanished, replaced with warmth that flooded her senses. He leaned closer, smelling of salt water and coffee. She trembled with anticipation.

The first brush of his lips was like a whisper. She pulled him closer and deepened the kiss.

"Nate," she breathed out in a sigh as he trailed butterfly kisses across her cheek.

"Meg, I almost lost you."

Being rescued by him sent a shiver of delight through her.

"What was I thinking? You need to get out of those wet things." Nate's arm snaked behind her, and he deposited towels onto her lap. "Start drying with these." He disappeared only to appear a minute later on the driver's side. He turned various dials, blasting hot air into the vehicle before he handed her a bundle of cloth and closed the door, leaving her dazed and confused.

The bundle contained dark-blue sweat pants and a hoodie with NAVY emblazoned across the front in bright yellow. Unsure what was next, she rushed to exchange her cold, wet clothes for the warm, dry ones. She was toweling her hair dry when he slid into the driver's seat.

He wore a matching sweat suit and had on tennis shoes. "Warmer now?" His eyes skipped across her as he glanced over his shoulder to back out of the parking space.

She nodded, wiggling her bare toes.

"Sorry I don't have any socks."

She laughed. "I can't believe you had two extra changes of clothes."

"Oh, I've got a whole wardrobe back there."

"Except socks."

"Except socks," he said.

She basked in his smile and teasing tone. Wrapped in warmth and contentment, Megan relaxed and let the tension leave her body. Exhaustion took over until she roused a bit to find herself cradled in Nate's arms as he carried her across the lawn. Snuggling against him, she mumbled her thoughts.

"Shhh. Go back to sleep." He eased her onto the sofa and covered her with an afghan.

But it was too late. The moment he walked out the door she was wide awake, the warmth of the Hummer replaced by the chill of the empty cottage. Rubbing her arms in an effort to warm them, she made her way through the bedroom. She turned the shower on as hot as she could stand it and let the heat soak through to her bones.

Twenty minutes later she emerged, somewhat thawed but still not warm. Sitting in a comfy chair beside her bed, she tugged on thick socks and a pair of boots. When she leaned back, she noticed her phone blinked red, indicating a text. In her rush this morning she had forgotten to take it with her, leaving it on the side table next to her chair. Good thing or it would be at the bottom of the Amelia River.

There were several texts from Sonia, who was anxious for an update on Emma and the Harpers.

Megan had pushed their disappearance to the back of her mind, telling herself that it was a misunderstanding or communications were down. She couldn't face the possibility that Mama and George were in danger as well. She could only pray that by the time they were able to get in touch with them, Emma would be home. "If we get her back safe and sound," she whispered.

But now she had hope. Today hadn't been a complete disaster—they had found the rest of the plants.

Her fingers flew across the screen of her phone.

Sorry, left phone at home today. Completed the ingredient list, but I won't be able to test it. Some of the plant samples were lost in the rain. It doesn't seem to make sense...

Someone banging on the door interrupted her texting.

Nate pounded the door again. The rain had stopped, sending the temperatures plummeting. He tugged at the collar of his coat against the bitter-cold wind howling off the ocean.

He regretted his rash actions earlier that day. Although Megan had seemed receptive to his kiss, he had taken advantage of her weakened state and allowed impulse to overrule sense. Needing to normalize the situation, he devised a plan. He would go to the cottage, cook a hot meal, and then they would sit down like rational adults.

And you'll apologize for your past behavior and ask her forgiveness.

He drew in a deep breath and blew it out. "Yes."

The door swung open. Megan took his hand and pulled him out of the cold into the cheery cottage. A fire gave off warmth and added to the coziness. She looked even more inviting in a soft blue sweater that added color to her cheeks. She welcomed him with open arms, and he wanted nothing more than to walk into them.

Here's the opportunity. Say something.

He turned several phrases over in his mind, but they seemed inane. His rudeness extended for years. How could one sentence make amends?

"Nate?"

He saw the challenge in her eyes and realized he stared at her like a lecher.

He cleared his throat. "Right. I'm making dinner." Pushing past her, he moved into the kitchen and unloaded the groceries from his duffle bag onto the counter.

"Do you need a cutting board?" Megan asked.

He took the one she offered.

She plucked up some red potatoes and began washing them.

This was not going the way he intended. He wanted to apologize with his actions, prove he wasn't the boor he so often portrayed. He took the potato from her and shooed her with his hand. "Sit down, and don't worry your purty li'l head about this," he said in an exaggerated Southern accent. *I want to pamper you.* He cracked a smile in her direction.

She followed his order, disappearing into the living room, but not before he caught a glimpse of the hurt in her eyes.

He rummaged through drawers until he found a knife and began dicing the potatoes with a vengeance.

Keep talking until she smiles.

He strode into the living room and found Megan curled up in an oversized chair that swallowed her. A picture of Emma lay in her lap. She looked up at him with blue eyes swimming in unshed tears. His defenses crumbled.

He pulled up the ottoman and sat in front of her. "Megan, we're going to find her. I promise."

Taking the picture, he looked at it a moment, then set it on the end table. He picked up her hand from her lap. The contact caused a pleasant tingle that he savored. Turning it over revealed the blisters on her palm from rowing. A sharp pain shot through his chest. He looked into her eyes, and for the first time he let his heart talk without filtering it through his mind. "Most days I lift weights, run several miles, and swim for hours in the ocean. The last two days were like a warm-up for me. But not for you."

She bristled in her chair, so he lifted her chin to make eye contact. "That's not a condemnation. You've been a trouper through all this. I couldn't ask more of a recruit."

He took her weak smile as confirmation that he was on the right track. "I would like your company in the kitchen ... and directions to your cabinets."

She uttered a shaky laugh. "I can't resist a man asking for directions." She held out her other hand and he pulled her out of the chair.

"What are we making?" Megan asked.

"Brunswick Stew."

"Yum. I'll bake some cornbread."

"C'mon. I'm starving." With fingers entwined, he led her into the kitchen. Soon the aroma of spicy stew filled the cottage.

Megan brushed the cornbread crumbs off the table into her empty bowl. "That really hit the spot."

"Yeah. We make a good team." Nate headed into the kitchen with a stack of empty dishes.

She wiped the table with a dishrag, smiling as she recalled bits of their conversation.

When Nate returned from the kitchen with the rescued backpack, she averted her face so he wouldn't see the color she felt creeping up from her neck.

"Some items were compromised due to the moisture." Nate spread the contents of the rescued backpack on the table.

Megan's mood sobered. "I still don't understand this formula. I can't imagine that this combination would be at all appealing." She picked up the puzzle page. The ink had blurred, and some of it was now illegible.

"When I got it to the house the seal was broken. The bag was full of water and all the plant samples were missing." Nate sounded as disappointed as she felt.

"Well, it's only been two days. I think I can remember all the plants. I just wish I had good samples and the time to test it. Maybe then it would make sense." She let out a deep sigh. "Let me start on the reconstruction." She disappeared and came back with a notebook and a Scrabble game. Sitting at the table, she wrote out the puzzle in the notebook. She had already unscrambled the plant names, and some of the positions of those letters had been circled—a puzzle within the puzzle.

She pulled out Scrabble tiles for each of the circled letters. Laying them out in a long line, she studied them, hoping something would jump out at her.

R B O T S T A K L T A H E E I R G D A T T R H N E I N T T H U S N U S T I F O U M E N O I E R E T T

When it didn't, she pulled out all the vowels: AAA EEEEEE IIII OOO UUU

This   left   her   with   the   consonants: RBTTSTKLTHRGDTTRHNNTTHSNSTFMNRT

She put together common consonant and vowel combinations, forming several small words.

AT AM AN I IN IS IT OR THE TO

Over the years, she had learned that the fun of doing these puzzles was letting the subconscious work, finding the solution when she wasn't concentrating on it.

Funny how the mind works.

Contemplating the remaining letters, she toyed with an E. She had used all the As. She still had four Es, but they were often in the middle or end of bigger words.

EEEE UU

TT STRN LD N F TR ST

THROUGH TKE

"The name of the perfume, Devastation, means destruction. Maybe the ingredients aren't supposed to smell good together," Nate said as he stood and walked toward her.

"Yeah, that's right." She swirled the remaining letters around the table.

"I keep thinking about those verses Dad wrote in our books. What if that's the message—devastation, destruction, Judas Iscariot, betrayal..."

He leaned over her shoulder to look at the letters. Then he reached out and created a word.

TRUST

A knock on the door shattered the silence. Nate opened it, and a blast of arctic air drove out the warmth of the cottage.

The same college-aged kid that had delivered the ransom note shifted from foot to foot in the doorway. "Delivery for Ms. Foster." He held out the envelope while edging away.

Megan raced forward at the sound of her name and snatched the envelope. Hands shaking, she ripped it open and stared at the cut out letters in various fonts and sizes.

Key meets lock to open door at live nativity on Centre Street 8 p.m.

Megan transferred her gaze to Nate and passed him the letter. "That's not fair! It hasn't been seventy-two hours."

"You expect a kidnapper to be fair?" Nate growled, crumpled the letter in his hand, and lobbed it across the room. "It's like he knows we've gotten all the ingredients."

Her glance fell on the Scrabble tiles as she wondered what the final puzzle would reveal. Megan's throat constricted. Was someone watching them?

"It's already seven-thirty," Nate said, interrupting her thoughts. He ripped the paper with the plant list out of her notebook. Grabbing their coats off the rack by the door, he tossed hers to her. "Let's hurry."

As they rode toward the historic district of the island, Nate laid out his plan. Megan would wander through the nativity scene until she was contacted. Nate would keep an eye on things from a distance.

Once parked, he kept a tight hold on her elbow as they joined the throng headed for the stone cathedral. When they reached the gates of Bethlehem, Nate pulled her aside and turned her to face him. "Focus on the mission. It's a simple exchange. I'm close by, even if you can't see me."

Megan took a deep breath and blew it out in a long sigh.

He squeezed her shoulders. "You can do this."

His confidence bolstered her. Determined not to let him or Emma down, she entered the living nativity scene with a buzz of anticipation running through her. Shepherds and village people milled around dressed in robes from biblical times. Surrounded by sheep and donkeys, Mary and Joseph watched over baby Jesus in the little half-stable built for the display. A weary innkeeper turned people away, directing them to his stable in the back. Peddlers approached visitors offering trinkets, food, and drink. Strolling past the inn with its roughhewn "no vacancy" sign, Megan started when a heavy hand grabbed her arm.

"Shhh. Don't draw attention."

A jolt went through her as she turned and saw baby-faced Miles Bentley. "You have Emma?"

"Come with me."

"Is she alright? You didn't hurt her, did you?"

"You have the formula with you?" His eyes darted to and fro over her head. He was only a little taller than her, but his iron grip told her his size was misleading.

"Yes, but ..."

"Good, we can't let them get it." He threaded her arm through his and pulled her away from the nativity scene.

"Where are we going?"

"We must stop them. Hurry."

"Stop who? Didn't you send the note?" Alarms sounded in Megan's mind.

"You can't give the formula to them," Miles growled.

"If you didn't send the note, then who are you? What do you want?" Megan tried to stop, but Miles was strong, pulling her along despite her resistance.

"I'm here to help you." They passed the crowds going toward the nativity scene, past parked cars, and onto deserted streets with sparse lighting. The echo of their footsteps rang through the brisk night air.

"Do you know where Emma is?"

"You'll never find her once you give them the formula. They'll kill her. It's what they do."

"Who? If you know who the kidnappers are, you have to tell me."

"It's better if you don't know. They killed a man in France. I'll explain everything once we're safe inside. I'm very close to solving this. Trust me. I promise I'm on your side."

Megan observed the man beside her—a study in contrasts. His short stature and round face gave him a youthful, innocent appearance, but his piercing blue eyes and sinister smile made her skin crawl. He was dressed in jeans and a sports jacket, making him appear normal. But his frizzy, strawberry-blond curls reminded her of a mad scientist.

The wind stirred Miles' jacket, and a glint of metal caught Megan's eye. A gun. Was it to protect or persuade her? Her feet slowed of their own accord as she scanned the area for any sign of Nate. Had he seen her leave with Miles? They had reached Harper

Scents. She could no longer see the crowds in the town square. Her screams would echo off the buildings but be lost to anyone who could help her.

"No, no, I can't risk Emma's life. I have to go ..." She had to get away, get back to the nativity scene where the kidnappers were waiting for the ransom. While Miles used the keypad and thumb print recognition to access the building, Megan took advantage of him releasing her to make a run for it, but she didn't get far. He grabbed her and shoved her into the building. "Quit making a scene. If they see us together, we're all goners."

A chill ran through Megan. What if Emma had been right here at Harper Scents the whole time? She and Nate had been here days ago. Could they have rescued her then? Why hadn't they thought to search the building?

Miles led her into the elevator and pressed the basement button. When it stopped, they walked down the long, dark corridor with only emergency lighting to lead the way. Their footsteps echoed on the tile floor as they made their way to the very last lab room.

"Have you been holding Emma in your lab?"

Miles gave her an odd look before turning away to punch in his personal code.

With a searching gaze down the hall, he opened the door. "Wait in here."

As Megan entered the dark room, a flash of light followed by a popping sound startled her. Before she could identify the sound, another shot rang out, the bullet whizzing past her face. Diving to the floor, she heard the loud report as Miles fired back. Then the door slammed shut.

Nate watched from a distance as a moon-faced man approached Megan, spoke to her, and they headed away from the nativity scene. He started following them, but the phone on his belt buzzed. He pulled it out and saw the call was from Paul.

"Speak," Nate said.

"I did some digging on that Miles Bentley you mentioned. Bad news—he's involved in corporate espionage, blackmail, and extortion."

"That sounds like our guy," Nate replied as he resumed following Megan, trying to keep her and the man in sight.

"They call him Baby Face Bentley, but don't let the moniker fool you. He's rumored to have a mean streak. In fact, he may have recently graduated up to murder. This is not someone you want to mess with."

"Got a picture?" Nate asked as he passed the last of the car-filled parking lots.

"Sure, I'll text it over now."

Nate glanced down at his phone when it dinged. "Got it. Thanks."

"No problem. Watch yourself, Harper. If you see this guy, don't try and take him on alone. Call me."

"Yeah, sure." Nate stood in the deserted parking lot and stared at the picture of the man who had Megan. Without the cover of the crowds, he had to let them go, but he assumed they were going to Harper Scents. He'd cut around the block and come up behind the building.

"Mr. Harper. Nathan? Is that correct?"

Nate groaned to himself as he turned to see two men. The one in jeans and a bomber jacket blended in with the crowd. His silver-haired partner wore a trench coat over his three-piece suit and stuck out a little more.

"Detectives." Nate struggled to remain pleasant. Megan was with that creep, probably the kidnapper, and he was stuck talking to the police. He didn't dare alert them to the situation. It could cost Megan and Emma their lives. So he played it calm.

"Leaving the party so soon?" Silva asked.

"Yeah. If you've seen one nativity, you've seen 'em all." He strove to keep his tone casual.

Silva leaned in and lowered his voice. "Maybe you're looking for a ... different kind of party."

Nate shrugged.

"Got a tip about a swap meet tonight. You know anything about that, Harper?"

Nate recognized the slang for a drug deal. "Can't say as I do."

"How about Emma? She hasn't picked up her ID yet." Benoit joined in, rocking on his heels.

"You know women. Too busy shopping." Nate side stepped the question, his stomach in a knot.

Benoit took a step closer to him. "Trouble seems to follow you, doesn't it?"

"Never has before."

"We get an anonymous tip, and here you are. How do you account for that, Harper?"

"Just lucky."

"I don't think so. In my experience, all the scenes make a movie."

"When that movie comes out, I'd like to see it." Nate crossed his arms. "Is that all detectives?"

Silva and Benoit looked at one another and then Benoit spoke for them. "For now."

Trapped!

Megan flattened herself against the wall behind the door. She didn't know who the first shooter was, but they seemed to be aiming for her and Miles. Now she didn't know where her protector was—or where Emma was, for that matter.

"Emma?" She whispered her sister's name and waited for any echo of a response. Silence filled the room. She slid down the wall until she sat on the floor and considered her options. Even if Nate had followed her, he didn't have access to the building. If Miles had survived the gun battle, he would have returned. She had to assume he was injured or even dead. On the other hand, the shooter hadn't come after her either. Were there two bodies in the hall?

She was on her own. A few days ago that would have terrified her, but her recent successes had boosted her confidence.

Think!

She still had the formula. Maybe if she headed back to the nativity scene she could negotiate with it for Emma. There were no sounds from the hall, but someone might be lying in wait. A small beam of light snuck in under the door and allowed her eyes to adjust to the darkness. She took advantage of it and searched for a weapon. Digging around in the drawers, she found a pair of tongs. She was familiar with lab equipment and figured that was the best she would get.

Armed, she listened at the door. All was quiet. She eased the door open and poked her head into the hallway, where an odd pattern of deep-red splotches thinned out into a single file trail.

Blood. Miles? Or someone else?

Megan skirted around the blood, sprinted to the elevator, and slammed her hand on the button. Then a terrifying thought popped into her head. *What if the shooter is still in the building?*

She jumped when the bell dinged, announcing the car's arrival. Flattening herself against the wall, she held her breath, waiting for someone to exit. As the doors started to slide closed, she threw her arm out and stopped them. Heart pounding, she peered inside.

A pool of blood and a hand smear down the wall, but no Miles. Why had he brought her down here? Was there a clue in the lab that could lead her to Emma? She hadn't seen anything. And who was shooting?

Megan backed into the far corner of the elevator and rubbed sweaty palms down her jeans, choking on the stifling air.

When the doors opened to the lobby, she peeked around and then sighed in relief. She bolted out into the chilly night and raced down the street until the sidewalks became populated. Only then did she stop to gulp air into her depleted lungs. Forcing herself to appear calm, she strolled to the nativity scene.

Twenty minutes later she stood in the middle of Bethlehem, frozen to the core. She stamped her booted feet and blew on her icy hands. She hadn't seen Nate since she returned. Either he had hidden well, or ...

She refused to finish the thought.

I shouldn't have left with Miles. But really, it wasn't her choice. He forced her to go with him. She put her hands up to her face, remembering the sensation of the bullet whizzing past her cheek. Swallowing hard, she tried to get rid of the lump in her throat that threatened to choke her. A tug on her jacket alarmed her and she jumped.

"Miss, do you have a key for my lock?" A rosy-cheeked boy held out a miniature treasure chest and looked up at her. The chest was locked with a tiny padlock.

Megan surveyed the crowd. In the shadows behind the crèche, a robed figure held a girl wearing a familiar dress. Her feet were bare and her hooded jacket cast shadows across her face, but she tugged away from the man, trying to break free.

Emma!

She looked back at the expectant boy. Miles said once the kidnappers had the formula, they would kill Emma. But there she was. Just yards away. Taking the treasure chest from him, she pulled down on the small lock and it opened. With trembling fingers, she worked the lock out of the latch and opened the lid. Inside was a note.

Fools rush in - Don't be one.

She glanced again at the robed figure. He gave a slight nod, and she fumbled in her jacket pocket for the piece of paper containing the plant ingredients. She slipped it into the treasure chest and gave it to the little boy.

The child weaved and bobbed around the legs of the adults in the crowd. As the boy got closer to his destination, the man shoved

Emma forward. While she made her way through the crowd with slow, inconspicuous movements, Megan remained frozen in place.

As Emma drew closer, it took every bit of discipline for Megan not to run forward to meet her. She tried to peer into her face, but the large hoodie hung low covering it. The sleeves fell far below her hands. Finally, Emma reached Megan and fell into her arms. Megan hugged her and covered her head with kisses.

"Honey, I'm so glad you're safe. Let's get you home and warmed up." She glanced across the green in time to see the robed figure limping away. She reached out and pushed the hood off. Although the girl staring back at her reflected Megan's blue eyes and blonde hair, even through the mud-caked face Megan was certain.

This was not Emma.

Chapter Nine

Monday, December 22, 10:00 p.m. – 28 hour remaining

After breaking away from Silva and Benoit, Nate strolled back toward the nativity scene. As the crowds thickened, shielding him from the detectives' prying eyes, he doubled back to the Harper Scents building. He eased around the corner into an alley and found himself face to face with a linebacker. The man's fist connected a glancing blow to Nate's chin, setting off an explosion in his head. Not waiting for the guy to take better aim, Nate ducked and plowed into his attacker.

The short, burly man had mass, but Nate had speed and training. He twisted the bull's arm behind his back and propelled him into the wall.

"Where's Emma?"

"Wo die Verwustung?"

"I don't think I like that answer." Nate growled and tightened his grip, jabbing him harder. "Where is she?"

"Nein, wirst du sie niemals finden." He rocketed off the wall, knocking Nate on his butt.

Nate rolled before the mammoth landed on top of him and then scrambled up to shove his foot into the slot between the man's chin and chest where his neck should have been. "Where did your boss take Megan?"

The man sneered at Nate.

A family walked by singing Christmas carols. Nate removed his foot and offered the man a hand up then pinned his back to the wall, pretending to dust him off. He didn't want to traumatize small children or draw the attention of the police. Not until he knew where they were holding Emma.

When the family passed, the man cocked his head toward the nativity scene. "Du narr. Go get your woman. We don't need her anymore." He pushed Nate aside and lumbered off.

Nate nursed a sore fist and watched him go. The man's size and accent matched what little Megan had been able to describe about one of the kidnappers. Half expecting to see Detectives Benoit and Silva, Nate surveyed the area for a loner who looked out of place, but all he saw were families and couples immersed in the scene. As the nativity shut down for the night, he spied Megan across the street arguing with a girl. He rushed over in time to hear part of their conversation.

"Please, she's my little sister. I'm begging you, help me find her."

"I'm sorry, lady. I don't know anything about a kidnapping. This is part of my audition for a movie role."

"The man you were with ... What's his name?"

The girl shrugged nonchalantly. "I don't know. Another actor, I guess."

"The agency who hired you?"

"I answered an ad in the paper. It was a cattle call. About fifty girls showed up. Then this big ox guy lined us up and compared us to a picture he had. I was picked."

When the girl saw Nate approach, she took off. He started to chase her, but she screamed and, while all eyes turned on him, she vanished.

"The formula?" He asked, turning back to Megan.

"Gone," she said, tears shimmering in her eyes.

"She did look like Emma."

Megan reached up and touched his cheek. "What happened to you?"

Her hands felt cool on his flushed face and he wanted to enjoy her caress, but he had to stay focused on the mission. "A distraction." He caught her hand and tucked it into the crook of his arm. "We'll sort this out."

He shortened his stride to match her smaller one, and they eased back to the Hummer in a thoughtful silence. Scenarios raced through Nate's mind as he tried to determine what the kidnapper's strategy was. The kidnappers had the formula, so there went their leverage. When they tested it and discovered it wasn't the next Chanel No. 5, Emma would die. He resisted the possibility that she was already dead.

They reached the Hummer and he helped Megan climb in.

He paused inside the door as she fastened her seat belt. "I'd like to look at the videos again. Did you delete them?"

"No, I thought they'd be evidence when... No. I still have them. What are you looking for?"

"I'm not sure. Something someone said. 'All the scenes make a movie.' Might be nothing, but I want to take a second look." He rounded the vehicle pondering the 'what ifs' and 'if onlys' of the last few days.

Megan huddled in the Hummer, letting the heat sink into her bones. Bright Christmas lights decorated homes and businesses along the way, adding to her melancholy. She should have demanded to see the girl's face before releasing the formula. Now they had nothing to bargain with. She cast a surreptitious glance toward Nate.

His face was drawn tight. Eyes forward, he ignored the twinkling lights. Both hands gripped the wheel with white knuckles. She imagined he'd like to wrap those hands around her neck for her stupidity. His kindness and compassion were more unbearable than his anger. She didn't know what he expected to find on the videos. It seemed a way to punish her for not protecting Emma in the first place. Her stomach churned, and she forced herself to take deep breaths to keep from being sick. Nate hadn't spoken a word since climbing behind the wheel, and she was certain he was seething and ready to lash out at her with the full force of his fury. She deserved whatever he said or did. She had given away the formula without securing Emma or ascertaining her whereabouts. Miles' warning echoed in her head. In effect, she had signed Emma's death warrant.

Nate broke the silence. "You left with a man and came back. What was that about?"

"That was Miles Bentley. I thought he was my contact, but turns out he was trying to get the formula for himself. He took me to Harper Scents and then there were gunshots—"

"Someone was shooting at you?" Nate cast a dark look at her.

"Weren't you there? You said even if I couldn't see you..."

"Yeah, well, our friends Silva and Benoit intercepted me. Said they were expecting me."

"They did this?" She raised her hand to his cheek.

He clasped her hand and brushed it with his lips before he continued. "No, that was our friend the sumo wrestler."

"From the alley?"

"Looked and sounded like the guy you described. Seems all the players were in town tonight and determined to keep us apart." He squeezed her hand. "I want to hear more about this shooting. How did you get away?"

The concern in his eyes was almost her undoing, so she looked down and concentrated on his large hand enveloping hers. Megan couldn't believe he wasn't angry with her, couldn't believe they had survived the events of the night. But here they were safe. Together. She concentrated on that thought as she told of the harrowing experience at the lab. She finished with a sigh. "But we didn't get Emma. I gave away the formula, and they're going to find out that it's no good. Then they'll kill Emma, and it will be all my fault. How could I be so stupid?"

Before she could gain an answer they arrived home.

Nate turned off the key and got out, while she remained in the vehicle, despair washing over her. When he opened her door, she numbly allowed him to release her seatbelt and lower her feet to the ground. Then he tilted her chin until their eyes met.

"You had to do a lot of thinking on the fly tonight. I can't say I would have done any differently." Drawing her into the comfort of his arms, he whispered, "We'll find her."

She leaned on his solid chest and drew from his strength. The steady rhythm of his heart against her ear spoke of his reliability. But another voice questioned why he was being so forgiving. She deserved his anger, his scathing sarcasm.

She eased out of his embrace and led the way to the cottage door. Once inside, she flipped up the laptop cover and clicked until she had the first video. She knew what it contained and dreaded watching it again, so she moved to the other end of the table and let Nate take the seat in front of the screen. To blot out the events of the evening, she emptied her mind and tinkered with the Scrabble tiles.

AM I IN IS IT THE TO

EEEE UU

STRN LORD NOT F THAN TAKE TRUST

BRGHT

In the background she could hear Emma's pitiful pleas for help, and her heart broke. Over and over Nate played the videos, and over and over Emma would beg for them to come rescue her. Finally, it stopped. He must have tired of hearing a cry that couldn't be answered.

"Are you making any headway?"

Megan looked up to find him observing her. His eyes held no trace of contempt. She still wasn't used to this new side of him, so she waited with apprehension for the old Nate to return. She marveled at how years of animosity had vanished in just a few short days. Their differences seemed so trivial in the light of Emma's kidnapping. Perhaps this was her chance for redemption. "Since the earlier clues were Scripture, I thought this might be as well, so I've been looking for that type of language."

Nate nodded. "Good strategy."

Megan studied the remaining letters.

EEEE UU

H MANS

B T R

R F G T

IT IS TO TAKE IN THE LORD THAN TO TRUST IN

"A lot of verses are comparisons or contrasts, so..." A few quick moves of her hand and Megan slid the final tile into place. "The puzzle says 'It is better to take refuge in the Lord than to trust in humans.'" She hunched over the table, frowning. "I don't get it. I was counting on this puzzle containing an extra ingredient or instructions to make those bad ingredients work. But this has nothing to do with a formula for Devastation."

Nate sat back in his chair, shaking his head. "It's a formula for life. He told us as much when we first found the puzzles. It was never about a perfume formula. He wanted us to work together, and this was his method to force it."

"But risking Emma's life? I don't believe George would do that for any reason."

"He never intended that. Remember, we found the letter about the formula and his will together in the office safe. We were supposed to get it when he died. The kidnappers must have found out about it, didn't realize his propensity for puzzles, and thought they had discovered a gold mine."

"Of course. Corporate espionage. Only they needed us to solve the puzzle," Megan said.

"I should have figured this out sooner. Dad did this all the time when I was growing up. He couldn't give a straight answer, had to be a riddle or an object lesson. A simple question was turned into an elaborate research project."

Megan covered her mouth with her hands, unable to stifle a yawn. "Why would he do that to you?"

"Actually, it was effective. I never forgot those lessons, because I found the answers for myself."

"But this time it backfired."

"Yeah, and we'd better find Emma before they realize that."

"So let's look at the videos again." Megan walked around the table and slid a chair next to Nate's.

He pushed the button to restart the video. "We're looking for anything out of place or a clue to her location."

"Okay." She tried to concentrate on the screen, but her eyelids grew heavy. Propping her elbows on the table and holding her chin in her hands, she fought the sleepiness she had lacked last night. If Nate thought the video held a clue, then it was vital that they find it. Time was running out and they were no closer to finding Emma.

Nate gave her arm a gentle shake. "Hey, you're falling out of the chair. Get some rest, lie down on the couch. I can do this."

"No, no." She shook her head and rubbed her eyes. "This is too important."

Nate lifted Megan's head off his shoulder. Careful not to wake her, he picked her up and carried her into the living room. After laying her on the couch and covering her with a blanket, he returned to the kitchen to retrieve the laptop.

Now he felt the same exhaustion. As he turned to sit in a nearby chair, Megan moaned in her sleep. He paused to see if she was waking before he sat and put his feet on the ottoman. Her eyes remained closed as she twitched and squirmed, reminding him of the night he sprinted her away from the crime scene.

Precious Megan. He had ridden roughshod over her the last few days. Not only through the grueling hikes and weather, but also through the guilt trip he had laid at her feet. He stole kisses, but he hadn't apologized. He led her on but hadn't spoken a word of commitment. An invisible force was drawing them together, blasting through his stony defenses to forge a stronger bond with her. If he didn't right his mistakes, this newly poured foundation would crumble. Even if an alliance failed, she still deserved more respect and compassion than he had ever offered her. It was selfish to guard his emotions at the expense of hers. He had seen the hurt in her eyes, knew the damage his cruel words had rendered.

His eyes grew heavy as he fought to keep them fixed on Megan. He didn't want her to be frightened should she stir. He glanced at his watch—after midnight—and tried to calculate how long he had been awake, but his fuzzy brain refused to focus. Thirty-six hours, no more than that.

There was something in the video he was missing, dangling just out of reach. He blew out a sigh of frustration. Maybe if he rested for a minute, it would come to him. But only a minute. He couldn't stop working until he solved this problem. He shut down the computer and rolled his head from side to side, easing the knots out of his neck, then leaned his head back and closed his eyes.

He who watches over you will not slumber.

That promise released him, and he drifted off to sleep.

Nate woke with a start. His legs were stiff and the cold seeped through his sweater. After stretching, he rubbed his arms to ward off the chill and glanced at his watch. *0500.*

He got up and stirred the embers in the fireplace then added a couple of logs. The dancing flames cast a warm light over the room. Kneeling beside the sofa, he allowed his gaze to linger on Megan, drinking in her beauty. Her sleep had deepened, the earlier restlessness replaced with peaceful breathing. His hand whispered over her forehead, brushing a strand of hair away from the healing bruise. The deep red had changed to a bluish purple.

He stood, bumping the coffee table in his haste, and strode to the computer, the niggling in the back of his mind coming into full focus. *Emma's bruise wasn't healing.* He expected to see the same torn dress and even the tear-streaked dirt, but the scratches and bruises should be healing. He flipped up the screen and muted the sound then replayed each clip in rapid succession. He buried his head in his hands.

Was Emma even alive?

Megan's eyes popped open, and it took a moment to realize she had spent the night on her couch. She stretched out her stiff back and eased onto her side. The flames licked up the logs in the fireplace, mesmerizing her as the nightmare came flooding back. It was over. She had given away their chance to bring Emma home safely.

She turned her head. Nate sat at the table and stared at the computer with a grim intensity. No sound came from the monitor, but she could still hear Emma's plaintive pleas. Guilt crushed her. It appeared he had been up all night trying to correct her error while she slept, indifferent to the damage she had caused. The least she could do was make coffee. She rose and went through the motions on autopilot.

When she came out carrying two steaming mugs, he looked up and she gasped. His handsome face was haggard, his skin ashen beneath his tan. She had never seen him looking so distraught.

"Nate? What did you find?"

"This wasn't done each day as it was sent to us. This is all one tape, one session. She's in the same dress, which isn't unusual, but she's in the exact same position. Your bruises are changing color and healing, but hers don't change at all. I'm certain it's one conversation." He rubbed a hand across his eyes and then fixed her with a sad stare. "It's been edited and the date stamp has been altered, but I think this was recorded when she was taken. There in the alley where you were found."

Megan sank into the chair next to him, willing herself to breathe. "What does that mean?"

"A video sent every day is proof of life, but if it was all filmed in the alley that night..." Nate slumped in the chair, defeat in his eyes.

Megan pressed her hands to her stomach in an attempt to squash the fear clawing at her. Nate had lost hope, so what chance did they have? Emma must be dead.

The video continued to run, and Megan sat straight up and leaned toward the computer. "Did you see that?" Megan reached out and slid the bar back then resumed play. "Right there." She froze the frame and zoomed in. "He looks familiar, I just can't..."

Nate's eyes narrowed and his jaw tightened as he leaned forward in the chair, staring at the reflection in the camera. "No. No, it's not possible." Nate slammed the laptop shut and grabbed Megan's hand.

She winced as his hand threatened to crush hers.

"Dad was right about one thing—trust no one."

"Who was it? Where are we going?"

Nate ignored her questions as he stuffed Megan into the cab of the Hummer, all the while running scenarios for the best strategy. *Direct confrontation or a flank attack?* First he had to take responsibility for his mistake. He had blamed Megan for Emma's kidnapping, when *he* had been the one feeding intel to the enemy. He cranked the beast before turning to her. "This is my fault. I trusted Paul Spears."

"What does Paul have to do with this?" Understanding dawned in her eyes. "Trusted him with what?"

"Emma's life." Not wanting to face her condemnation, he slammed the vehicle into gear. The Hummer sped down the quiet, residential streets still blanketed by predawn darkness.

"No cops. You're the one who said we absolutely couldn't tell the cops." The hurt in Megan's voice pierced his soul.

"When I got the first couple of letters, I thought it was related to work." He blew out a breath. "Devastation sounds like a military operation, so I considered it a bid to buy military secrets."

Nate ran a hand over his face. "I met Spears during war games about five years ago. He was a special agent with NCIS. My crew took his team down on a dive. We hit it off, became friends. Then a couple of years ago, he was injured on the job."

"He told me about it at the picnic."

"That's right. You've met him. Standup guy. Top level security clearances, even in the private sector. So I went to him with what I had every reason to believe was a military intel problem."

"But then Emma was taken."

With a hasty glance at the deserted roads, Nate roared through the intersection, ignoring the flashing red light. "According to the video, he took her. The thing is, he warned me they'd take it up a level."

"You're still talking to him? When?"

"Yesterday. I asked him to check out Miles Bentley. He called with the info right after you left with Bentley. Said he was a corporate spy."

Megan tugged on the seatbelt, turning so she could look directly at him. "So Miles is working with Paul, who knew we had all the ingredients. They wanted to test it before releasing Emma. That makes sense, but who was shooting at me and Miles?"

"I don't know. An accomplice, probably." Nate careened onto the expressway.

"I waited a long time before I snuck out of the lab, and then it was twenty minutes or so before the little boy contacted me at the nativity scene. Paul could have been the shooter."

"Maybe Bentley was pulling a double-cross. Paul warned me not to take him on alone."

Silence filled the vehicle until Megan whispered, "Now they know the formula is worthless."

Refusing to contemplate defeat, Nate swallowed the lump in his throat. "There must be evidence in his office as to Emma's location. We've gotta hustle to beat the office staff." Nate pressed down on the gas. His stomach boiled like a pot of water as they sped into Jacksonville through light holiday traffic.

Megan's hands lay folded in her lap. She had her eyes closed, and her lips moved without uttering a sound. Only the white of her knuckles gave away her anxiety.

Nate whipped into a Park-N-Ride lot on the outskirts of the city. In silent agreement, they boarded the monorail that rocked and swayed over city streets as it took them into the heart of downtown. Nate took Megan's hand as they exited the train across the street from the high-rise that housed Spears Security Consultants.

They entered the lobby and skirted a massive pyramid of poinsettias. Riding the elevator to the twenty-third floor, Megan prayed no one would be in the offices to stop them. The elevator doors opened to a spacious foyer flanked by conference rooms on each side. The large mahogany counter housing the receptionist's desk was centered in front of a wall bearing a gold SSC logo. Megan peered down the left hallway to a row of offices that seemed to form a horseshoe backing up to the receptionist's desk. Across from the offices were restrooms, a water fountain, and the door to the stairwell.

Nate motioned for her to follow him down the right hallway. "We've got maybe an hour before staff starts showing up."

"I smell coffee," Megan replied in hushed tones. "So maybe not."

"Take cover." Nate pushed her back.

"What's the matter?"

"Paul's in his office."

Megan's heart sank. "What are we going to do?"

"Create a distraction." Nate surveyed the room.

Megan looked too. They were in the break room that backed up to the restrooms. The glass wall looked into offices opposite. Not a very good hiding place. "What kind of distraction? A phone call or the fire alarm?"

Nate shook his head. "He'll ignore a fire alarm. I need enough time to find evidence linking him to the kidnapping."

"So if a coffee pot exploded and made a huge mess..."

Nate grinned. "That works."

Megan poured the contents of the full pot over the counter and floor and then placed the empty pot back on the hotplate. Nate pulled her behind the receptionist's desk.

Nothing happened.

"How long?"

Megan shrugged. "Depends on how weak the glass is."

"Grr... Stay here." Nate disappeared and reappeared in the doorway to lob the coffeepot toward the counter. The glass crashed into pieces as Nate dived back into their hiding spot.

"What in the..." They heard Paul sputter a stream of expletives followed by the sound of paper towels being ripped from the dispenser.

Nate and Megan flew down the left hallway to Paul's office. As Megan slid into the huge, leather executive chair and began tapping computer keys, Nate rifled through the credenza and desk drawers.

"Whacha got?" he asked.

"I'm opening every file that leads to sub-files and sub-sub-files. So far, nothing."

"It's not going to take him long to clean that up, if he even bothers." Nate closed a drawer and stood behind her.

"Pay dirt," Megan said.

He looked over her shoulder at the list of folders including Devastation, Letters, Centre Street, French Connection, and Scuba Camp. "Great. But we need hard copies or he'll erase it."

"No problem. I'll zip the file and e-mail it to myself." Her fingers flew across the keys. As she hit the send button, Nate slid a paper under her nose.

The key doesn't open the door. The lock will be destroyed. The clock is still ticking.

The style matched all the other letters. Their eyes met.

Nate snapped a picture of it with his phone. "I found it in the credenza. That seals the deal. Paul's our man."

"He's going to kill her."

The silence was deafening until the ding of the elevator broke the spell.

Nate shoved the letter back where he found it.

Megan scrambled to close the files she had opened.

When she finished, Nate grabbed her hand and pulled her into the corridor, where he glanced around the end of the wall. A well-groomed woman stepped off the elevator. He ducked back behind the wall, keeping Megan on his six.

"Lydia!" Paul called out. "The stupid coffee pot exploded. Can you finish cleaning this up?" His voice neared where they were hiding. If he came back, they'd be caught red-handed.

Nate leaned around the corner to see if the coast was clear and motioned for Megan to dash across the hall into an empty office. As they ducked behind a potted plant, Paul walked into his office and stared at the computer for a moment. Nate froze. Had they left something awry? Then Paul opened the drawer of the credenza, the same one Nate had been snooping in, and pulled out a folder. A frown crossed Paul's face, and he glanced at the office where they were hiding. Nate willed himself not to move or breathe. He could feel the tension radiate from Megan as she did the same.

BRRING.

Megan jumped at the jangle of the phone, bumping into Nate. He wrapped his arms around her waist to steady her. Paul must have hit the speaker key, because he talked as he put on his suit jacket, took some papers from the folder, and placed them in his inside coat pocket.

"Read his lips," Nate whispered.

While they both focused on Paul's mouth, he leaned over the computer to shut it down, hit a button on the phone, and walked out of the office—right past them.

"I'll strangle him," Nate hissed and lurched forward.

Chapter Ten

Tuesday, December 23, 8:00 a.m. – 6 hours remaining

"No." Megan grabbed Nate's arm and pulled him back behind the plant. "Emma needs you."

And so do I.

She stroked his back until his breathing slowed.

"Let's get out of here before I change my mind." He pointed to an exit sign on the wall, stealthily opened the door, and they scurried down the stairs.

Nate led the way with Megan close behind. As they raced around the corners of each flight, dizziness set in. She slowed but kept moving forward. As her legs turned to jelly, she missed a step and grabbed the handrail for support. Nate was around the bend and out of sight. She took a deep breath and tried to catch up to him, but her lungs were bursting for air. She rounded the next corner. Seeing the big "10" on the sign by the door, she redoubled her efforts. *More than halfway down. You can do this Meg.* She descended two more flights before her resolve faltered. Sweltering in the confined space, she clung to the rail and wheezed. She couldn't take another step.

Poking his head around the corner, Nate saw her distress and bounded up the steps to join her. "Let's take a break." He wasn't even breathing hard.

Unable to argue, she bent over with her hands on her knees. "Can't we catch an elevator?"

"And if the doors open and Paul's inside?"

"Good point."

"We're safe here." He leaned against the railing. "Sit down and catch your breath for a minute."

"No," she panted. "We've got to take what we've found to the police."

Nate shook his head. "Not until we know where Emma is and that she's safe. We've got to keep playing his game until then. He's planning to contact us again, so he still wants the formula. We'll demand true proof of life."

"But there's no time." Megan's lip quivered as she began moving down the stairs once again.

Exhausted and breathless, they exited the stairwell into a side hall of the lobby. As they hurried toward the main entrance, Nate did a sudden about face and steered her back down the hallway, into a coffee shop.

"Wha…" Megan tried to protest, but Nate pulled her in tight against his side, falling into line. When the person ahead of them finished ordering, he stepped up to the counter. "I'll have a big, black coffee. No latte, no shots, no odd flavors—just strong coffee."

The barista gave him a patronizing look and translated the order back to him.

"Yes, and a couple of those," he added, pointing to some pastries. "Honey, what do you want?" He looked down at her with an odd expression.

Confused, she followed his lead and placed an order.

After paying, Nate led her along the counter and glanced out the shop window.

"Paul came off the elevator," he said in a low voice. "There he is." He pointed with his chin. He pulled out his cell phone and raised it with the camera pointed at Paul.

Paul approached the ATM and withdrew money. Then he placed a white, business-sized envelope and the money into a larger envelope. Crossing the lobby to the courier office, he slipped the large envelope into a drop box.

Nate snapped pictures of the sequence of events.

As Paul glanced in their direction, Nate and Megan ducked their heads. Megan turned her head under Nate's arm and watched Paul exit the building. "He's leaving. Shouldn't we follow him?"

"Too risky." Nate shook his head. "We could lose him, or he could spot us. Better to sort through this information for something that will help."

The barista called their number. Nate picked up the order while Megan found a table.

When he joined her, he pulled a stack of brochures from his jacket pocket and spread them on the table. "I found these scuba camp brochures in his credenza, under the letter." He shook his head. "He always asked about Emma. I told him she was bugging me to teach her to dive." He pushed back in the chair. "It never occurred to me that he was capable of this."

Megan pulled out her phone and began perusing the files she had confiscated. "Atlantic Dive Camp in Key West," she read.

"Got it." Nate pulled a threefold pamphlet out of the stack and waved it at her.

"Paul sent them emails claiming to be a security consultant for Emma's father. The camp started Saturday."

"Says here, this week's for families vacationing in the Keys over the holiday. Parents are expected to pick up their kids by 1400 hours on the twenty-third." His finger underlined the words as he read.

"That explains the seventy-two-hour deadline."

"Paul's headed to pick her up, but he still doesn't have the formula. His plan is falling apart."

Megan's heart rose in her throat. "What will he do with her? Where will he take her?"

"He'll be desperate." Nate rose from the table and tossed his coffee cup in a trash can. "We've got to get her out of that camp before he does."

"It's an eight-hour drive to Key West." Megan looked at the clock on her phone. "We've only got five."

Chapter Eleven

Tuesday, December 23, 9:00 a.m. – 5 hours remaining

*F*ive hours.

There was only one way to get from Jacksonville to Key West in that amount of time.

"Does Dad still have the company plane?" Nate asked.

"Sure, but…"

Nate pulled out his phone. "Let's see if I'm still on the authorized list." As they waited for the monorail to take them to their car, Nate punched up a number in his phone. "Hey, Bobby. Nate Harper. Can you get the plane ready for takeoff in about an hour?" He listened for a moment and gave Megan a thumbs up. "Yeah, we're headed down to Key West to pick up Emma."

"Key West? I thought Emma was spending the week with a friend here," a familiar voice said.

Nate's stomach churned as he turned to face Detectives Silva and Benoit. "What are you doing here?"

"We could ask you the same thing."

"We had some business to tend to," Nate said, pulling Megan toward the turnstile.

"Right, with Paul Spears. Only you didn't stay long enough to talk to him."

"Are we under investigation for something?"

"Funny you should ask, 'cuz we are working a case, and every time we get a tip, you two show up." Silva rocked back and forth on his heels.

The monorail rattled overhead as it pulled into the station.

"There's our ride. Gotta go." Nate pushed Megan up the escalator ahead of him.

Benoit shouted up to them, "Run away now, but we'll find the connection."

"Three hours, four at most," Nate shouted over the plane's roaring engines. "We'll make it."

Megan gave a mute nod as the radio crackled with clearance for takeoff. Nate plunged the tiny six-seater down the runway. Gaining speed, the tin can rattled and vibrated until she was convinced it would come apart at the seams, but then the wheels lifted off the ground and it rose high into the sky. She put aside her reservations about the size of the plane and about Nate's ability to operate it as she watched the buildings beneath her grow smaller. Finding Emma was more important than her personal fears or discomforts.

"Don't worry, Megan. I have thousands of hours of flying experience in all types of conditions. We have clear skies, so we won't run into any bad weather." Nate set about explaining the various instruments and what role they played in navigation. As they flew south, he pointed out the landmarks below them, keeping her updated on their progress down the coast.

Megan sighed and released the seatbelt from her clutches. Despite the fact that his friend, Paul, had betrayed him, she had full confidence in Nate. And she had a confession of her own to make.

"I considered contacting Paul—I thought a private investigator could help us without the kidnappers finding out."

Nate looked at her through narrowed eyes. "Sooo, you're not angry with me?"

"I'm furious that he took Emma and then took advantage of your friendship to keep tabs on us. But I'm not angry with you."

"Good. I need you on my side." His smile sent a warm flush through Megan and she turned away, pretending to be mesmerized by the cloudless blue sky. Through this nightmare, she had seen Nate's true character, which was even more attractive than his physical good looks.

"Why didn't you ever mention hiring Paul?" Nate asked.

"Sonia thought it was a bad idea." She took a deep breath. *Might as well make a full confession.* "You remember Sonia from the company picnic? Well, she called and could tell something was wrong. I wasn't going to say anything, but I—I was scared to death and you were angry with me. I needed someone to confide in."

Nate reached over and covered her hand. "I was scared, too. From now on, let's confide more in each other."

Glancing at his work-worn hand, she remembered how he had caressed her face, drawing her in for a sweet, tender kiss. The memory sent a pleasant tingle rippling through her.

"I'd like that." She turned her hand over, intertwining her fingers with his.

"I've misjudged...

Suddenly the bottom dropped out from under her, launching her stomach into her throat. Nate jerked his hand out of hers, gripping the wheel as he fought to maintain control of the plane. She noted his smile had faded, replaced by a tense frown of concentration. There were no clouds in the sky, no thunderstorms. Had he forgotten a critical inspection or checklist item? They had loaded up so fast, urgency overriding sense, so it was possible. She pursed her lips at him before she looked out the window. They continued to follow the coastline. Would it be better to land in the ocean or on land? Her stomach churned as the plane dropped again.

"A little turbulence from the jet stream," Nate said. "I'll get us clear of it in a minute."

His voice had a calming effect, and her jangled nerves began to settle down. If only she could get the nausea to do the same. She leaned forward, wrapped her arms around her stomach, and took a deep breath, willing it away.

He gave her arm a reassuring pat, but she shook her head. "Wheel ... hands on wheel."

"It's called a yoke." He chuckled. "And it's okay. We're out of it now."

When he withdrew his hand, she was sorry. She underestimated the immense comfort and pleasure his touch provided.

As the plane leveled out, Nate checked the navigation maps and noted the time. Right on schedule. They would soon be rescuing Emma.

Unless Paul's already taken her. He refused to contemplate that possibility. Failure was not an option.

He cast a covert glance Megan's way. She seemed calm, now that they were out of the turbulence. It was time to clear the air between them once and for all.

He cleared his throat. "Coming home after Dad and Carol got married was weird for me. I was angry at him—at everyone, but even when I got over that—"

"There were strangers in your house."

"One particular, very pretty stranger." He risked a glance in her direction, and she rewarded him with a toothy grin. "In my line of work I analyze intel, process facts. Emotions don't come into play, so that situation was very confusing for me. I just didn't want to deal with it and I handled it badly. It's not an excuse..."

"I know what you mean. Whenever you were coming home for a visit, I was a nervous wreck. I wanted you to like us, accept us, but I really wanted you to *like* me and I felt so foolish for that."

PING

Megan's smile faded. "What was that?"

"Not sure." As Nate examined the various instruments, the pinging continued. He tapped on the fuel gauge. It registered half full, expected for the hour and a half they had been in the air.

"Everything alright?" Megan asked, unease lacing her voice.

"It's probably nothing," Nate assured her. A moment later, the right engine sputtered.

"That doesn't sound like nothing."

Nate picked up the radio. "Mayday, mayday, mayday. This is November-fife-niner-ait-bravo-golf requesting emergency landing. Over."

"November-fife-niner-ait-bravo-golf. This is Titusville Airpark. What is your emergency? Over."

"Titusville Airpark, we seem to have a fuel problem. Over."

The right engine continued to sputter and then quit altogether.

"November-fife-niner-ait-bravo-golf. We have a turf field runway one-eight-right cleared for landing. Over."

"Titusville Airpark. Update. We've lost our right engine. Confirming cleared for landing runway one-eight-right. Out."

Glancing out the window, he noted the left propeller was slowing, giving the illusion of spinning backward. He eased down the nose of the plane to prevent a stall.

"We're going to be fine, but put your head down. It might be bumpy." He gave what he hoped was a reassuring smile.

Nate searched the dense tree cover for a break big enough to land the plane and then rechecked their location. It should be in view by now. Why wasn't he seeing it?

The left engine sputtered to a stop, leaving them gliding with no power. He had the situation under control, but only if they found a clearing soon. Crashing into the thick, pine forest below would be disastrous. The plane would be destroyed, and their probability for survival was slim.

He gripped the yoke tighter and continued to scan the area. Just in time, a clearing revealed hangars and planes, identifying the airfield ahead. He pulled back on the throttle, slowing the airspeed until he located runway eighteen. He prayed for safety as he took the plane into a sharp descent.

The small craft bounced on the rough turf, and Nate fought to slow it as they rapidly approached the tree line. Lurching to an abrupt stop whipped his neck back. He released a pent-up breath and turned to Megan, who still had her head between her knees.

"Hey." He touched her shoulder. "It's over. We're safe."

His heart sank when she raised her head, tears streaming down her face.

"We'll never reach Emma in time now."

Before he could think of anything positive to say, a knock on the window interrupted him, and then the cockpit door was yanked open.

"Y'all alright in there?" An older man with thinning gray hair slicked back from his forehead appeared in the doorway.

"Yes sir, we're fine." Nate climbed out of the cockpit.

"Name's Rusty. Rusty Nales." He wiped his hand on his grease-stained uniform pants before sticking it out in front of him.

Nate accepted his outstretched hand. "Nathan Harper."

The man gave his arm a workout and released it to poke his head into the plane. "Missy, you look mighty shook up."

Nate pulled the man aside. "Do you have a mechanic here?"

Rusty studied him for a moment. "Don't know as he's available."

"See, we're supposed to be picking up our little girl from the Keys. And well, she's waiting with no way for us to contact her..."

"Ahh, I see why the missus is upset. I reckon I can help y'all." He ambled over to the plane, whistling a tune.

"You're the mechanic."

Rusty nodded without missing a note. He examined the engine for a few minutes and then walked back to the wing.

Nate joined him. "It seemed like something with the fuel line."

Rusty pulled a small plug, drained some liquid onto his finger and sniffed. "Yep. That's not fuel, it's water."

"Water? No wonder she went out so fast."

"Too much for normal condensation. Some places water down their fuel. Best keep an eye on 'em from here out."

"Can you repair it?"

"Yep. Gotta tow motor. We'll pull it over to the hanger yonder." He tipped his head toward the building. "Drain the tanks and refill them. You'll be right as rain in no time."

Rusty showed Nate and Megan to a small waiting room and office. Nate's offer to help resulted in a nod toward a sign listing the cost of customer interference. Rusty's garage was his castle, and strangers were forbidden. As Rusty went whistling into the adjoining hanger, Nate paced the small waiting room.

As the wait stretched out, Nate's mind descended down a dark tunnel. Losing Emma would send him into a tail spin he might never recover from.

Why, Lord? When will the losses stop? Nate stopped in the middle room with arms akimbo.

My grace is sufficient for you.

Megan watched as Nate paced up and down the tiny room. His restlessness did nothing to calm her nerves. Seeking a distraction, she pulled out her phone and scrolled down to Paul's files she had emailed to herself. The file titled *French Connection* drew her attention. Inside, she found Paul's escape plan.

Nate took the seat beside her. "Rusty here's slower than molasses."

"You're beginning to sound like him." She handed him the phone. "Look what I found. Paul Spears has already contacted a perfumer in France who's willing to manufacture the Devastation formula for him. According to his timeline, he expects to be a billionaire overnight."

"That's a powerful motive. He's convinced we gave him a fake formula and he's holding out for the real one, but his hideout for Emma has run out. So what's his next move?" Nate got up and paced again. "His original plan was to get the formula, and then he'd tell us where she was—safe and sound at a dive camp having the time of her life."

"But how did he get her there? If he took her himself, she could identify him."

"Unless he 'rescued' her from mammoth man."

Megan cocked her head to one side. "Maybe. I'm sure they covered her head, like they did mine. So maybe she never saw Paul as one of the kidnappers."

"Right. She would have trusted him to drive her to the dive camp. Especially if he told her it was my Christmas gift to her." Head down, Nate paced away from her.

"Okay, but if his plan was to reveal her location in exchange for the formula, then escape to France, how was he going to explain knowing where she was all this time, without telling us?"

Nate wheeled around, stabbing the air with his index finger. "Good point. Once we got Emma back and she told us he drove her to the dive camp, we'd know he was involved."

"Maybe he just didn't care. He'd be in France making billions of dollars, so it would be easy to change his appearance and identity."

"But now he doesn't have the formula, and his hideout for Emma is gone."

"He could leave her here and still go to France. He'd be safe there, out of our reach." Megan said.

Nate shook his head. "No, the US has an extradition treaty with France. He wouldn't leave behind a witness."

"Then his only choice is to take her to France with him." A shudder ran through her as stories of kidnapped young girls hidden in basements for decades filled her mind.

"That's not his only choice," Nate said.

An even more chilling vision entered Megan's mind.

Rusty appeared at the doorway, wiping his hands on a greasy, red rag. "All set, y'all."

Megan stared at the plane while Nate paid the bill. She was terrified of climbing back into that deathtrap. What if the fuel wasn't the problem? Or what if there was another problem?

Be of good courage...

Squaring her shoulders and taking a deep breath, she pushed down her fears. Emma depended on them.

Nate swung into the pilot's seat and went through the checklist. When he finished, he fired the engine to life and aimed the plane down the runway.

Megan closed her eyes as they bumped and jostled down the turf, this takeoff far scarier than the one in Jacksonville. As they left the ground, her anxiety turned from her fear of flying to the upcoming challenge. She alternated between checking her watch and searching the ocean below for the chain of islands. Would they make it in time, or had the mechanical problems given Paul enough time to beat them to Emma?

Nate's furrowed brow and intense concentration said he was thinking the same thing. She wasn't sure if that was comforting or concerning, but at least they were in this together. She couldn't imagine having to go through this ordeal alone.

"Look." Nate pointed out the window. "There's the Overseas Highway."

Megan peered out at the thin ribbon of road sitting atop the blue ocean interspersed with areas of varying shades of green. Lurking under the water's surface, small sections of land protruded out to form islands. The Florida Keys.

The plane banked and began its descent.

"And there's Key West."

Megan looked out the window expecting to see a lush green island with a few quaint bungalows and beach shanties. She panicked at the sight of a bustling metropolis with every square inch covered with buildings.

"It's a city!" She looked at him, her eyes wide. "How will we ever find Emma?"

Chapter Twelve

Tuesday, December 23, 1:00 p.m. – 1 hour remaining

Nate circled the small plane in for a landing. "We don't have to search the whole island. Thanks to your computer skills, we know which dive camp she's at. It's just a matter of beating Spears, and we've got a head start on him."

"Except we lost time with the water in the gas tank. Could Paul know we're on to him?"

"I don't see how. Even if he saw us, he wouldn't have known what plane we were taking."

Megan glanced at her watch. "Only one hour until the deadline."

The plane landed with a satisfying bump on the tarmac, and Nate taxied it to a stop. It seemed to take forever to deal with the airport procedures, but eventually they were able to hail a taxi. As Nate gave the driver the address of the Atlantic Dive Camp, Megan peeked at her watch again.

"We'll be there in no time," Nate said, settling into the seat. "The whole island's only seven square miles."

Megan sighed with relief. He was right. How long could it possibly take?

Famous last words.

Nate regretted his casual assurance. For some unknown reason, the street was a parking lot. Craning his neck, he tried to determine the problem, but a semi loaded with an oversized yacht blocked his view. Megan's fidgeting betrayed her anxiety and he had to admit, his was rising. He leaned forward. "What's the hold up?"

The driver shrugged. His island time attitude didn't extend to kidnappers and deadlines.

Nate repressed the desire to force some urgency onto the driver. "Where's the dive camp?"

"Straight up this road, about three miles, maybe a little more."

Three miles was too far to make a run for it like they did in the movies. As frustrating as the traffic was, they were better off waiting. Nate wrapped his arm around Megan's shoulder, giving it a reassuring squeeze. "We'll make it." He kissed her forehead and hoped he spoke the truth.

His nerves were wound tighter than before any Navy mission he had ever been on. *Lord, there's so much more at stake here.* Forcing himself to regulate his breathing, he prayed for wisdom and envisioned a successful result. While Megan watched the traffic in front of them, his mind ran through scenarios they might encounter and how he would deal with each one.

By the time they pulled into the parking lot of the brightly-painted motel, he was calm. Nate paid the driver and then performed a visual reconnaissance of the area of operation. A balcony with rooms off of it ran around the second story of the concrete-block building. Stairs were located on the north and south end. A large pool surrounded by deck chairs filled the courtyard.

To the right, they entered the office, which opened into a dining room—probably the restaurant when this had been an actual motel. Now it was a cafeteria for the campers. Nate scanned the space for signs of Emma, but the only person he saw was a young girl with a winter tan manning the front desk. A name tag identified her as Caitlin.

"We're here to pick up Emma Harper. Do we have to wait until 1400 hours?" Nate asked.

"No sir. We can have her here in a few minutes. They're still on the boat, but Cody will bring her in by Jet Ski." She indicated the motorized personal watercrafts lining the dock.

Nate was getting antsy. What if Megan was right and the fuel delay had given Spears time to catch up to them? Megan looked as anxious as he felt, so he gave her a wink in an effort to appear casual and relaxed, as well as to prevent raising suspicion.

"Trying to get that last dive in, huh?"

Caitlin gave him a brilliant smile. "They went to Joe's tug this morning."

Nate chuckled. "Old Joe. I've been there. It just sits there on the ocean bottom, upright, like nothing ever happened."

"There's a few stories floating around, but nobody's claiming responsibility. Especially not Joe."

"I'm trying to recall that exact location. Close to Toppino's Reef?"

"Not far." Caitlin pointed to the location on the map under the glass countertop. "It's a good dive for beginners. Just sixty-five feet of water, and there's a lot of marine life—spotted morays, barracuda, and horse eye jacks. Even a Jewfish named Elvis."

Nate grinned. "I know she's having the time of her life. I hate to take her away."

Caitlin clicked a few keys and then frowned. Clicking a few more keys, she raised her head and presented Nate with a stiff smile.

"I'll need to see some ID from each of you."

"Sure. Glad you're taking precautions to keep our girl safe." Nate pulled his wallet out of his back pocket. He hoped the change in her demeanor was his imagination on overdrive.

Megan stepped up to the counter. "I'm Megan Foster. My purse was stolen, and I haven't had a chance to get everything replaced."

"No problem." She kept Nate's license while she typed information into the computer.

This time, Nate was sure the smile was forced. A moment later the phone rang, and Caitlin's guarded responses confirmed Nate's suspicions. Something was terribly wrong. He casually moved behind Megan and massaged her shoulders. "We'll have our baby home soon, honey." He leaned forward and whispered in her ear. "Do you trust me?"

Her muscles stiffened under his hands, but she nodded in assent.

He took her hand and led her toward the side door, just as Paul Spears limped in through the entrance.

"You can't outmaneuver me, Harper. Where's the real formula?"

"You'll never get away with this, Spears." Nate glared at him.

Megan pulled her hand free from Nate's and charged toward Paul. "I know it doesn't make sense, but this is where the clues led us. Please, this isn't worth killing over."

"You're a bright girl, Megan, but holding back vital information? That's not smart. You're the one putting lives in jeopardy, not me."

The insinuation in Spears' voice drove Nate to land a right hook across the man's jaw.

Spears took a couple of steps back before regaining his balance. "Tsk, tsk... Seems you don't value Emma's life as much as I thought," he said, rubbing his chin.

Nate grabbed a handful of Paul's shirt, pulling him close enough he could feel the man's breath on his cheeks. "Don't you dare touch her."

Megan placed a hand on Nate's arm. "Not until we have Emma back."

Nate wanted to pound Spears into the ground, but Megan was right. At least until they had Emma in their custody. He shoved Spears away from him.

Paul smoothed the front of his polo shirt and scoffed. "Better listen to her."

With Caitlin's suspicions aroused and Spears on the scene, their only chance was to get to Emma first. They couldn't wait for her to be brought to them. Nate grabbed Megan's hand and headed out the door only to be greeted by the large moose of a man he had battled in the alley at the nativity scene.

"Otto may help change your minds," Paul said.

Nate pushed Megan to the side and lunged toward the linebacker, then dodged him at the last minute. He grabbed his beefy arm and threw his leg across the backs of his knees. The giant went down. Brushing himself off, Nate rose and pushed Megan out the side door.

"Go after them, you big oaf!" Paul roared in disgust as Otto peeled himself off the pavement.

Nate yanked Megan down the dock and jumped onto a two-man Jet Ski.

"Untie it," he said as the engine sprang to life.

Megan unhooked the rope and tossed it up on the dock. Scrambling onto the back, she wrapped her arms around Nate's waist. "Go!"

Chapter Thirteen

Tuesday, December 23, 2:00 p.m. – Out of time

Megan clung to Nate's waist as the Jet Ski slammed up and down on the choppy waters. Occasional glances back revealed that Otto had also commandeered a Jet Ski and was gaining on them.

"Hurry!" She patted Nate's chest with urgency.

Otto zoomed around on their left, spraying water over them and cutting in front. Nate released the throttle and turned sharp to the left as Otto circled them on the right. The small water craft rocked violently on the wake.

Nate pulled her hands tighter around his waist. "Got a good grip?"

Not waiting for her answer, he revved the engine, daring Otto to come closer. Then he shot forward, just missing the front of Otto's

Jet Ski and sending it backward into the water, dumping its driver on the way.

Megan looked back to see Otto wrestling with the capsized vessel.

When Nate released the throttle, Megan popped her head up over his shoulder. A diving boat floated nearby. *Emma.* They had beat Paul and his henchman and were going to save her.

Nate steered the Jet Ski alongside the boat and dropped out the grapnel anchor.

"Hello, welcome aboard!" A middle-aged man with leathery skin helped them onto the deck. He wore his graying hair pulled back into a ponytail. "I'm Ted Owens."

"This is Megan Foster," Nate said as he helped her board the boat. "And I'm Nathan Harper." He extended his hand, and Ted shook it.

"My wife, Jenny." Ted motioned toward the athletic woman by his side.

While Nate exchanged pleasantries with the couple, Megan looked around the boat.

"A Sea Eagle, 60-foot aluminum dive vessel." Ted bragged on its components. "She doesn't have sleeping berths, but we have a galley and a table down under."

Her eyes searched through faces of teenagers on vinyl-covered benches. The canvas roof sheltered them from the bright rays of sunshine, but the contrast of shade and sun made it difficult for

Megan to see. Plus, some wore masks. Along the sides of the boat were tanks and scuba gear, and off the back was a small platform where the divers re-entered the boat.

Megan looked out at the gentle waves and wondered what had happened to Otto. With half an ear, she listened to the conversation between the two men.

"...not her father," Ted was saying.

"I'm Emma's brother."

"Yes, she spoke of you, rescue swimmer ... Navy?"

"That's right," Nate said.

"She said you're the reason she wanted to learn to dive."

Nate nodded. "I gave her the manual and promised to take her with me once she was certified."

Megan watched as the two men sized each other up. Ted seemed to be leaning in their favor. If Emma trusted them, it made sense that he would release her to them.

Jenny put her hands out in front of her. "Please understand our position. The main reason Paul Spears chose our camp was because we don't allow any personal phones, computers, or social media. He's called our office every evening, and we allowed Emma to talk to him as a special concession because of the situation."

Ted rubbed his hand across his jaw. "You see, when Mr. Spears brought Emma here, he explained that he was a security consultant for George Harper and that she was the subject of a nasty custody battle. He warned us that you and Miss Foster might try to take her. Now, you seem on the up and up to me, but after what I just saw on the water..." He glanced at the ocean before looking back at Nate and then Megan.

"You have to be careful who you hand her over to. I appreciate that, and I understand that you're getting conflicting stories. How can I convince you I'm the one telling the truth?" Nate asked.

Before Ted could respond, a head popped out of the water. "Dad!"

"What is it, Cody?"

"This camper, she's tangled up in some fishing line. I can't get her loose."

"Jenny, bring me some gear." Ted zipped up his wet suit. "This problem is getting kinda old. Careless fishermen leaving spent line in the water. They don't know—or worse, don't care—how dangerous their invisible litter is to divers." Ted donned a tank and goggles and dove into the water.

"Is she a novice diver?" Nate asked, turning to Jenny.

"This week is her first..."

Screams erupted from the far side of the boat, followed by a commotion.

"Hey, get out of here," one of the boys yelled as Otto jumped into the water.

"Does that guy work for you?" Megan asked.

Jenny shook her head. "I've never seen him before. Jimmy, where did he come from?"

"He climbed in over the side of the boat and took my tanks," the boy replied.

"He's the one who was chasing us on the…"

Before Megan could get the words out of her mouth, Nate kicked off his shoes and dove in, disappearing beneath the azure water.

"He doesn't have any equipment. How will he breathe?" Megan looked at Jenny, who seemed to share her alarm.

"Once he's down, he can share air with Ted and Emma, if she has any left."

"Emma? It's Emma that's stuck?" Megan rushed to the side of the boat, knelt and leaned over the side to search the water.

Cold water penetrated Nate's street clothes, stinging his bare skin as he kicked with powerful strokes toward the ocean floor. As he glided through the water, he assessed the situation. Cody and Ted huddled around Emma. They seemed to have the situation under control, but where was Otto?

A moving shadow interrupted the streaming shafts of light. Nate turned as Otto swam hard toward him, spear gun in hand.

They don't teach this in AIRR school.

He knew the man's brute strength, but he had also learned his weaknesses. For one, he wasn't a thinker, rather relying on his size to intimidate his opponent. That size was a penalty in the water, plus Nate had a definite advantage in training and experience. His goal was to lead Otto far away from the rescuers so their work could go on unimpeded and they could get Emma onto the boat.

Otto bore down on him, aiming the gun. Instead of engaging, Nate swam under and past him, then turned to face him. Otto glared down the shaft of the spear gun and fired. Nate somersaulted in slow motion, like an astronaut. The arrow drove past him, vibrating as it struck the sandy bottom. Nate thrust forward and slammed into Otto then wrestled the spear gun out of his grip.

While they circled like Sumo wrestlers, Nate maintained a safe distance from Otto and looked for vulnerabilities. Otto's eyes seemed focused on the spear gun rather than on Nate. Testing this theory, Nate held out the weapon and grabbed it back as Otto took a swipe at it. The beast showed no signs of wearing down, and the tank on his back provided all the air he needed to keep attacking. Nate had to level the playing field.

He tossed the spear gun aside and as Otto swam toward it, Nate maneuvered behind him and stripped the air tank from his shoulders. The regulator yanked Otto back, his arms and legs thrashing. Nate tore the mouthpiece away.

Otto spun behind Nate, floundering for a moment.

Nate's lungs burned and his vision blurred from the lack of oxygen. He took advantage of Otto's floundering and locked onto the mouthpiece, drawing in a deep breath that filled his lungs with life-giving air. He turned toward Emma's direction and found her swimming along the sand with Cody beside her.

Ted gave Nate a thumbs up sign.

Nate was shrugging into the stolen tank when Otto rammed him from behind, ripping the regulator from his mouth. Bubbles burst upward, upsetting a school of neon-colored fish. Darting every which-way, they obstructed Nate's view. When they cleared, Otto was lunging toward him with a knife. Nate kicked hard to propel himself backward, but the water made his movements sluggish.

Otto swung his arm, catching Nate's bare foot with the sting of the blade. Then he shot upward and plunged the knife toward Nate's heart.

Nate threw up his arm in defense, and the knife buried deep into his forearm.

Otto continued to hold him, pure hatred radiating from his eyes as he twisted the knife.

Grimacing in pain, Nate probed for a weak spot on his opponent. He knew he could hold his breath longer than Otto, but the blood flowing from the stab wound was considerable. Sharks would smell it and gather for a feeding frenzy in no time. As Nate reached the limit of his endurance, a paralyzing cold seeped into his bones.

Chapter Fourteen

Megan and Jenny peered over the side. The boat rose and sank with the gentle waves, and although the water sparkled clear blue on the surface, after only a few feet visibility was lost. They could see the white churning, indicating a fight of some sort took place below, but they couldn't see who or what was happening. After what seemed an eternity, a head popped out of the water.

Otto looked at the two women, and then he swam toward the Jet Ski that Nate and Megan had ridden.

"No," Megan cried. "Where's Emma?"

Jenny wrapped an arm around her. "I'm sure that those three will have her freed in no time. My husband is very experienced, and Nate is a rescue swimmer. They'll be fine. You'll see."

"What's that?" Megan asked, pointing at a red stream rising to the surface.

Jenny gasped. "Hands in the boat everyone." She ran over to where the students sat under the canvas. "I don't want anyone to panic. We may see some sharks in a few minutes. Be very careful, keep your hands in the boat and no one will get hurt."

Megan moved behind her. "That really is blood then."

"Yes. One of them could've gotten scraped on some coral."

Megan turned back to look at the bloodied waters. "I don't know ... that seems like an awful lot of blood for a scratch." She leaned over the railing and searched for some glimpse of the divers. "How fast will the sharks come?"

Jenny pointed over her shoulder as a fin broke the surface and then disappeared.

Megan clenched the railing and closed her eyes and prayed. "Bring her here. Bring her here," Jenny said, turning to the dive platform.

Megan's eyes sprung open.

Ted and Cody handed Emma up into the boat and then hauled themselves in.

Flying across the deck, Megan embraced Emma. "Oh baby, I'm so glad we found you."

"I'm fine, Megan. I was worried about you. Paul said you were alright, but he wouldn't let me talk to you or see you, so I was scared he wasn't telling me everything."

"No, no. Nate found me right away. We were so worried about you." Megan pulled back to examine Emma for cuts and scratches.

Finding none, she laughed in relief. "Look at you. You're safe and you're not hurt."

"You didn't know where I was? Paul said..."

Megan shook her head. "It's okay, it doesn't matter. We're together now. That's all that matters." Ignoring the tears streaming down her cheeks, Megan stroked Emma's hair, brushing wet strands out of her face. The sense of relief was overwhelming.

"Excuse me, ma'am." The camp medic approached. "I need to give her a quick once over."

"Of course." Megan stepped back as the medic led Emma below deck. Turning to share her joy with Nate, she realized he wasn't there. "Where's Nate?"

Ted shook his head. "He's been cut." He looked at the bloodied waters. "I saw the first shark and knew I had to get the kids to safety." Ted studied the water as more fins appeared.

Jenny protested. "I know you want to help him, but there're too many sharks. You may not even reach him before you're attacked."

Dread filled Megan. She didn't want Ted to risk his life, but she didn't want Nate to die either. If he was the source of the blood, then what chance did he have?

"Yes, but we have to give him a fair shot." Ted grabbed a fire extinguisher, pulled the pin, and tossed it over the opposite side of the boat. "That should draw the sharks over here and give Nate a chance to come up."

Megan and Jenny joined him and watched as the sharks swarmed to the bait.

"I hope that's not dinner you're throwing overboard."

Megan swirled around. "Nate!" Without thinking, she flung her arms around his neck. She didn't care that he was dripping wet.

He embraced her, patting her back and whispering soothing assurances.

She could hear his heart pounding beneath his wet clothes and knew that he had battled hard to survive. She could have stayed in his arms forever, but she remembered the bloody water. Drawing back, she found the blood streamed from his arm. His face was ashen from the loss of blood and lack of oxygen, but he remained steady as a rock.

"What happened down there?"

"Otto got lucky." He looked at his arm. "But not as lucky as he wanted."

"He took off on the Jet Ski," Megan said. "Do you think he'll be back?"

"Not if he's smart."

Ted called down to the medic who was examining Emma. He came up and cleaned the wound on Nate's arm and foot while Nate described the fight with Otto.

The medic finished and advised Nate to see a doctor about stitches as soon as they reached shore. As Nate thanked him, Emma came up from below deck. She had changed from her wet suit into shorts and a T-shirt. She ran across the deck, and Nate scooped her up in his good arm. He held her until the blast of a ship's horn broke them apart.

"This is the police. Prepare to be boarded."

Chapter Fifteen

Emma and Megan clung to one another as the police herded the trio onto their boat. A rotund officer met them on deck and promised a tour of the boat, to which Emma enthusiastically agreed.

Nate sighed in relief. For all the trouble he and Megan had gone through to solve the puzzle, the most frightening thing had been out of his control. He had envisioned Emma being held in dark, dank quarters, bound and gagged, fearing for her life. Those thoughts had shaved some years off his life, but seeing her unscathed by the trauma gave him mixed emotions. Although he appreciated Paul's clever kindness of stashing her in such an idyllic setting, that didn't get him off the hook with Nate. Spears was still a greedy, ruthless kidnapper. If they hadn't discovered him, it was certain the next phase of his plan would have been more diabolic.

The boat rocked on the waves as it approached its mooring, bringing Nate out of his reverie. They debarked and entered the

Key West Police Station, at which point they were split up, each going into a different office.

Nate wasn't worried. Of course the police wanted to speak to everyone individually. But once their stories all meshed—and they would—the police would understand that Paul Spears was the bad guy and they would release Emma to Nate and Megan.

The uniformed officer escorted Nate down the hall and indicated a room on the right. Nate entered the bare room, its only furnishings two chairs on opposite sides of a table. The officer nudged Nate toward the chair farther from the door. A legal pad and pen lay on the table.

"It'll save time if we can get written statements from everybody," the officer said and left the room, slamming the door behind him.

Nate surveyed his surroundings. With so little to see, he spied the cameras in each corner of the ceiling at once.

An interrogation room?

He was expecting an interview, not an interrogation. Taking into account that there were three of them in a moderately-sized police station, he reasoned it was probably the only room available. This stark environment would be terrifying for Megan or Emma, but he was used to it. And he often performed training classes in front of cameras, so those didn't bother him either.

Nate tugged at the borrowed Atlantic Dive Camp T-shirt that fit his biceps too snugly. He was tired from too many sleepless nights, and the underwater battle had taken the last of his reserves. Shifting on the unyielding metal chair, he focused his exhausted brain on the facts.

A few minutes later he laid down his pen. He reviewed his neat, block-print statement. Satisfied that he had covered all the salient points, he stared into the camera as if to say, "I'm done. Let's get this show on the road."

A moment later a detective walked through the door.

Nate slid the legal pad toward him. "When can we take Emma home?"

"Patience, Mr. Harper." He studied Nate's written statement. "When was the first time you heard about Devastation?"

"A few weeks before the kidnapping, I received a riddle. I thought someone was opening dialogue to purchase military secrets. I ignored it, figuring they'd go after an easier target."

"Didn't you sign a counterintelligence brief at your enlistment stating that you'd report any such contacts to your commanding officer?" The detective flipped a chair around and straddled it, crossing his arms on its back.

"Yes, but it wasn't clear that's what it was."

"How did Paul Spears come into the picture?"

Of course they had interrogated Paul. Nate wondered what story he had fabricated, but it didn't matter. As long as he stuck to the truth, it would all come out in the wash. He had nothing to hide. Only his pride would be damaged, no thanks to his gullibility.

"I was having lunch with Paul the day the letter arrived, so it came up in conversation. I guess that wasn't as coincidental as I thought." Nate ran a hand over his head. "When the second letter arrived a week later, it was more threatening. Nothing specific, very vague. I shared that with him as well."

"What did Paul suggest?"

"He was very adamant that I take the letter seriously."

"But you didn't."

"I went through my files. I didn't have anything. Spears was supposed to be checking with his buddies at NCIS." Nate readjusted in his chair.

"It never occurred to you that it was related to Harper Scents?"

"Look," he sighed, "I've never had a very high opinion of the perfume business. It was nothing but a pain in my neck, and I kept as far away from it as possible." Nate leaned forward, elbows on the table. "I couldn't fathom that a formula for perfume was worth someone's life."

"But you realized it when Emma was kidnapped. Why didn't you contact law enforcement?"

"Spears was law enforcement, a former special agent with NCIS, a security consultant, and he was already familiar with the case. Why wouldn't I have trusted him over strangers?"

The detective stared at him without uttering a word.

Nate struggled to remember anything that would have given Paul away. A word. An action. But he couldn't think of anything that he would consider suspicious. What explanation had Paul given? Why would he do this to Emma?

The officer leaned forward. "So he was your ally, your confidante, and then boom! You didn't trust him. You decided he was behind the kidnapping, and through some divine inspiration you discovered where Emma was being kept and rushed down here in the nick of time."

"It's in my statement." Nate pointed at the document. "I spent hours reviewing those videos. And then I saw it. Actually, Megan saw it—Paul's reflection in the camera."

"But we don't have access to those videos."

"Sure you do. They were emailed to Megan. We didn't erase them."

"Humph..." The detective kicked back his chair and strode out of the room.

After several minutes of waiting, Nate stood and paced the small room. Why couldn't they just take Emma and go home? Or at least to a hotel where they could all get a good night's sleep.

At the sound of the door opening, he turned on his heels to face a tall woman with spiky salt-and-pepper hair that emphasized a large frame covered in lean muscle.

"I'm Detective Sam Brantley. I have a couple of forms for you to sign." She settled into the other chair and slid two documents across the table.

Nate glanced over the pieces of paper. *Right to remain silent. Right to an attorney.* He looked at Detective Brantley. "What's going on here?"

"Standard procedure."

For an arrest!

"You don't have to talk to me, but if you sign the second form, we can get all this cleared up and..." She let the sentence dangle.

Nate looked at the second form. *Waiver of rights.* What had Spears told them? "Okay, fine. I have no reason not to talk." He scrawled his signature across the page, confident he could refute any lie Spears had concocted. He shoved the paper across the table. "Where's Emma? Is she alright?"

"She's fine. Dr. Serrano is counseling her." She placed an electronic tablet in front of him. "I need you to explain these."

Nate stared in disbelief at emails from his account to Paul Spears. As he swiped the screen, his disbelief turned to horror. Black-and-white evidence that he masterminded the plot to kidnap Emma in exchange for Devastation.

Detective Brantley leaned back, rested her elbows on the arms of the chair and templed her fingers. "You hated the fact that Megan, this interloper, was getting an equal share of your inheritance. It ate at you for years."

He held the electronic tablet in his hands and shook his head. "I didn't want any part of the business."

"Right." She sat up and leaned in again. "But then you learned about Devastation, a formula worth millions. You didn't have to manufacture it, and you could sell it on the black market. It was the perfect revenge. Only, dear old dad had set it up so you had to work with Megan to get the formula. That's when you concocted the kidnapping scheme."

"I would never jeopardize Emma—"

"But you didn't. You held her captive in paradise. It really was the perfect plan." She stood and walked around the table then sat on the edge of it next to Nate. "You needed an accomplice, and Spears fit the bill. Your military training and Spears' NCIS training combined covered all the bases." She circled behind him. "Now you only had to wait for the right timing. When the parents went away, Emma was left in Megan's care. You used her guilt and fear to manipulate her into doing your bidding. 'No cops,' you told her, and she believed you. She trusted you. Maybe she even fell for you. Her big, strong, military hero."

Brantley's words echoed his thoughts. Somewhere down the hall Megan was being presented with this same scenario. She would hate him. For years she had tolerated his coldness and sought to bring reconciliation. Now she had succeeded, only to learn that their truce was a lie, a cruel manipulation.

"Was it worth it?" Brantley asked.

Nate shook his head. "I didn't mean to hurt her. I ... Well, it turns out she's not who I thought she was."

Brantley sat down across from him and lowered her voice. "And that was the hole in your plan. You realized you loved Megan. You wanted to call it off, but Spears wouldn't let you. You're not a bad guy, but seeing your inheritance being stolen ... that'd make me mad. And when we're mad, sometimes we make bad decisions. But it shouldn't ruin a life, shouldn't rob a teenage girl of her big brother. Charges haven't been filed ... yet. Let me help you turn this thing around, make this what it really is—a family spat that got out of hand."

"If you really believe these emails..." Nate raised the tablet toward her. "...then why are you offering me a deal?"

"Are you planning to make kidnapping a career?" She didn't wait for an answer. "Our prisons are already overcrowded. We don't need to waste space on a guy like you, who, as I said, made a mistake. No, Spears is the real bad guy here. I mean, his only motivation was pure greed, right?"

She removed Nate's written statement from a folder and placed it in front of him. "Modify your statement. Show us how Spears coerced you. He's the one we really want. He's already under investigation for drug possession. Your statement on the kidnapping charge would seal a conviction and get a true criminal off the street."

Nate stared at the paper. So this was how it felt to be judged on appearances and false evidence. Why was Megan so kind to him all those years, when he refused to see the truth? Refused to even give her a chance.

"Don't take too long. This deal has a short expiration date."

Nate picked up the pen.

Megan surveyed the small office where she had been deposited, separated from Nate and Emma. Safety posters hung on the walls, nautical charts covered the desk and a large window opened onto the hallway. Police in uniforms and plain clothes passed by, none seeming to care that she had been left here unattended.

Finally, a guy stepped into the room. Sun-bleached hair hung down in his eyes and spilled over his collar. Loosening the tie from his thick neck, he stood staring at her for a long time as he tapped his pen on a notepad. Having assumed the police were their allies, she fidgeted as condemnation radiated from the man towering over her.

"What's going on? Have you arrested Paul Spears?" Megan asked as her thoughts raced. Maybe Ted and Jenny were involved in Paul's kidnapping scheme. They seemed so nice, but...

"I'm Detective Ashton Ryder." Sitting, the detective laid the pen down and leaned forward, elbows on the desk. "It's a custody issue, really. Once we determine who has legal guardianship of Miss Harper, everything will be fine."

Megan licked her lips. Neither she nor Nate had legal guardianship. Would the authorities be able to contact Emma's parents? They would be worried sick about her.

Detective Ryder flipped through the scribbles in his notebook. "Mr. Spears states that Miss Harper's parents are on a cruise and he was to escort her to and from the dive camp in their absence."

"No."

Ryder raised one eyebrow.

"I mean..." Megan shook her head. "They always take a vacation for their wedding anniversary. They close down the business the last two weeks of the year, and Emma spends the week of Christmas with me. So yes, her parents are supposed to be on a cruise, but we haven't been able to contact them, and they're not on the ship's manifest."

The detective ran his index finger across his chin as if waiting for her to continue.

What was she supposed to say?

He studied his notebook again. "You claim to be Miss Harper's sister? Is it Miss or Mrs. Foster?"

The confusing last names again. "Half-sister. We have the same mother."

Ryder nodded, continuing to saw his chin with his finger. "Why didn't you contact the police when Mr. Spears took Miss Harper?"

Guilt flooded through Megan. This was her fault. She was the one who had allowed Emma to be kidnapped. "I thought we could find her if we just did as the kidnappers asked. I didn't care if they were caught or not, as long as we got Emma back."

"That was a bad decision—one that could have far-reaching consequences."

Had she and Nate unwittingly committed a crime by not reporting Emma missing?

"I didn't know what to do. I mean, I was kidnapped too."

Again, the single eyebrow lifted.

"I didn't know it was Paul, err, Mr. Spears."

The detective sat back in his chair, so Megan went through the whole story of that terrible night. As the terror took over, she could feel the stifling gunny sack that had covered her head. To combat her fear, she forced herself to turn off her emotions. Impossible as that seemed, it was necessary to save Emma. She told the story as she would if she were giving a report to the board.

Beating out a rhythm with his pen, Ryder spoke. "So, instead of enlisting the help of the police, who are experienced in these matters, you went off like a couple of vigilantes or rebel heroes."

"Paul Spears was helping us ... or at least we thought so. He was an expert at this sort of thing. He advised us to do exactly as the kidnappers asked. Isn't that what the police would have done?"

"Except the police would have been present at the drop and nailed the guy."

"But we didn't care if they were caught. We just wanted Emma safe."

"Nate brought Spears in. He convinced you that it didn't matter if the kidnappers were caught. And he stonewalled detectives Silva and Benoit."

She stared at her hands, fingers entwined, twisting and turning. She couldn't turn on Nate—she loved him too much. He had done what he thought was best, and who's to say he wasn't right? They might have wasted valuable time answering questions like this while Paul got away.

"Tell me about Devastation."

"It's a formula for a perfume. The kidnapper, Paul, demanded it as the ransom. Only there was no formula. We had to find the ingredients, and when we did, the result didn't make any sense."

"Think back to the very first time you heard about it. Careful now. Who first mentioned it to you?"

She bowed her head and whispered, "Nate."

The detective reviewed his notes, shuffling papers. "Let's talk about the nativity scene. You turned the formula over to a little boy and a girl who looked like Emma was released to you?"

"Yes."

"And someone was holding this fake Emma until you placed the formula in the box. Can you describe him?" Ryder asked.

"Tall, thin. I couldn't see very well. It was dark, but he..."

"Was Nate with you?"

"No."

"But he reappeared as you were arguing with the girl, allowing her to escape. Very convenient." Leaning across the table, the detective drilled her with a piercing stare. "I want you to think real hard. Are there other inconsistencies in Mr. Harper's story?"

Megan's heart pounded and heat rushed up her face. Was the timing suspect? Where had Nate been when someone was shooting at her and Miles Bentley?

Ryder's phone buzzed. He glanced at it then left the room, abandoning Megan to her doubts. Could Nate be involved with Paul? How had he known about the kidnapping and arrived there so quickly? She dropped her head in her hands. No, she wouldn't believe what the police were saying. She had to remember some fact or clue that would absolve Nate beyond all doubt.

A ruckus in the hall brought her head up in time to see a uniformed police officer leading Nate away in handcuffs. She jumped up and ran to the window, banging on the glass. "Wait! What are you doing?"

The officer looked in her direction with a frown and a shake of his head while Nate kept his face and eyes straight ahead.

When the detective returned to the room, she spun around. "What's going on here? Where are they taking Nate?"

"Sit down, Ms. Foster. It's all right here." Ryder held up a file folder.

She crossed her arms and stared at him for a moment before letting out a sigh and returning to her seat.

"We found these emails between Harper and Spears." He opened the folder and shoved it across the table.

Incriminating words flooded her brain as she stared at the printed form.

"Harper planned this whole thing," Ryder said.

She laid her hands on both sides of the folder. "No." Megan stared at the words, but they blurred together.

"When the formula turned out to be a dud, Spears turned on him."

Megan shook her head as she picked up the papers and shuffled through them. "No. No. No."

"Look at the facts. You weren't hurt during the kidnapping. You got a little bump on your head but nothing serious."

Megan laid the papers back on the table and folded her hands in her lap. She made eye contact with him and gritted her teeth. "Nate would never hurt Emma."

"And he didn't. We've talked to Emma. They must have drugged her because she woke up 'rescued' and Spears brought her to the scuba camp for 'protection' while he and Harper supposedly looked for the kidnappers. She was told you were fine, healing from some minor injuries."

Megan pursed her lips as she tried to process everything the detective was telling her.

"I'm sorry Ms. Foster, but these are the facts. We've arrested Nate Harper on kidnapping charges."

Chapter Sixteen

Nate flinched as the bright light flashed in his eyes.

"Turn left," ordered the police officer operating the camera.

At least Megan and Emma are safe.

The authorities had made it clear that Paul Spears was going away for a long time. His financial records revealed he was buried in debt. Thanks to the phone records and the files Megan had found, law enforcement knew he'd already been shopping the formula around top fragrance manufacturers in France. Even if he managed to escape the kidnapping charges, they had surveillance of him dealing street drugs. Spears was no longer a threat.

Nate rubbed at the black ink on his fingers. The frame around him was vice-tight. He shouldn't be surprised. One of Paul's specialties was hacking into various computer systems. Paul knew the types of things law enforcement would look for, and he'd made sure they were there. Nate had refused to take the deal that had him admitting to kidnapping Emma. To make that clear, he had added 'This is a true and accurate account of the events' to his statement.

Still, something didn't feel right. He just couldn't put his finger on it.

Emma burst through the door, wrapped her arms around Nate's waist and squeezed him tight. "They can't keep you here, Nate. You're innocent. I know you are. Tell them." She sobbed into his chest.

Nate folded her into his arms, rocking her side to side. "Hush, sweetie. It's okay. Everything's going to be okay."

When he looked up, Megan stood in the doorway. He froze. How she must hate him. He wanted to rip Spears limb from limb, so she must feel that and more toward him. She must believe he had played her, the ultimate manipulation. Especially after...

He eased out of Emma's embrace, wiped the tears from her cheeks, and placed a tender kiss on the top of her head. "Sweetie, let me talk to Megan for a minute."

As Emma slipped out of the room, Nate braced himself for the blast he deserved. It was what he would deliver if the tables were turned.

Megan continued to stand in the doorway. Tears shimmered in her eyes. And then, to his surprise, she was in front of him, arms wrapped around his neck. "Nate, we'll get you out of here. I'll call Sonia. We'll get the best criminal attorney."

He pulled back from her and held her upper arms. "You're not angry with me?"

She shook her head.

"Do you understand what I'm charged with? Do you understand that I don't have a defense? Do you understand that they're saying I used you, manipulated you, betrayed you?"

"The evidence they have looks bad, but I trust you. You couldn't—wouldn't—betray me or your family."

If the shoe were on the other foot, would he be as forgiving? He had confided in Paul and look where that got him. And yet, an unshakeable faith filled her eyes.

Forgive as I have forgiven you.

He pulled her arms from around his neck, placing them at her side. "After the way I've always treated you and now this? You don't need to help me."

"Nate." She cupped his face in her hands and pulled him down for a kiss.

He remembered how sweet her kisses were, longed for that connection with her, but he cared too much to put her through another ordeal. He was facing a trial, possible jail time. And, although he was innocent, he wasn't sure he would escape the trap that ensnared him. Megan would stand by him through anything, but he couldn't ask her to. He covered her hand, turning to press a kiss against her palm. "Go on now. Take care of Emma. She'll need extra attention."

Ryder cleared his throat. "Ms. Foster, it's time to go."

She held Nate's gaze a moment longer, then dropped her hand, turned and disappeared. Standing at military attention, he waited for the door to close, leaving him alone with only her memory.

Megan couldn't get out of the jail fast enough. She had to get in touch with Sonia ASAP. When the guard buzzed open the lobby door, she found Ted and Jenny Owens sitting with Emma. As she approached the trio, she motioned for her sister to join her.

"What's going to happen to Nate?" Emma trotted to catch up.

Megan didn't have an answer. Nate denied needing her help, but she had seen the evidence and it was staggering. His stoicism convinced her that he understood the gravity of his situation. He required top-notch legal assistance to have a fighting chance. She pushed through the door and stopped, dazzled by the sunlight.

Emma followed her out. "Where will we go? What will we do?"

"We'll figure something out." Megan gathered her into her arms.

"We feel horrid about all of this." Jenny stood in the doorway. "Come home with us."

Megan held her hands up in front of her. "Oh, we couldn't impose."

"We live at the hotel. Camp closed at two, so we have all those empty rooms. Besides, where else can y'all go?"

Megan chewed her bottom lip. Where else indeed? She had no transportation, no money. Besides, in spite of what he said, she couldn't leave Nate here to fend for himself. No, she had learned a lot about perseverance this week, had realized an inner strength she didn't know she possessed. Now was not the time to quit.

She squared her shoulders. "That would be wonderful. Thank you."

After a quiet dinner, Megan and Emma retired to their room. Once settled, Megan called Sonia.

"It's so surreal," she ended her brief synopsis of recent events, "but at least I have Emma here with me safe and sound."

"Nate? They arrested Nate?"

"Yes, and I really need to get him a good attorney, fast."

"I hate to kick a guy when he's down, but I had a funny feeling about him."

Megan smiled and it felt good to have the load of worry lifted. "I could tell by the way you went after him."

"Yeah, he's one fine specimen of manhood. But to be honest, he can be a little scary, and I'm not saying that just because I'm a scorned woman. Although you have to admit the man was crazy to turn me down."

"Well, he's got fortitude, I'll give him that. Because you are a force to be reckoned with," Megan said.

"Okay, I admit I can get a little carried away, but the arrogance of that man. And a control freak. I can't believe he hasn't made a play for the company sooner."

"Nate's innocent, Sonia. He'd never hurt Emma." She glanced up as her little sister came out of the bathroom, towel drying her hair. Wanting to avoid upsetting her, she lowered her voice. "In spite of all his bluster, he's an honorable man. That's why I need to get him a good attorney. Do you know anyone?"

"Sure, I'll give you some names. But listen, don't tell Nate they're from me. We didn't part on the best of terms, and he'd blow a gasket if he knew you had consulted with me."

"Thanks, Sonia."

After hanging up, Megan called several of the attorneys Sonia had recommended, finally finding one in town and willing to take on a new client on Christmas Eve. He promised he'd go to the jail to meet with Nate and discuss the arraignment.

As Megan finished up the call, Emma curled up on the sofa beside her. "Do you want to talk about it?"

"I was very scared when it happened, but when you told me that God was with me I felt better. In my head, I kept singing that song from church about never being alone."

"I'm so glad you were comforted by God's presence. That's what I prayed for." Megan rubbed light circles on Emma's back.

"The police said there was a video and asked if I remembered making it. I didn't then, but now ... I don't know. Maybe. There were bright lights in my eyes, and I remember reading from a big white poster board. I didn't know it was a video. I don't even remember what I read."

Megan knew all too well what she had read. The thin, broken voice played in her mind.

"I feel awful that you and Nate were worried about me when I was having so much fun."

"I'm glad you were having fun." As she held Emma close to her, Megan's memory flashed to some of the horrible scenarios she had imagined. She breathed out a long sigh of relief. "And I'm glad you made that video, even if you didn't know it at the time. Honey, that's how we discovered Paul Spears was the kidnapper, and that led us to you."

"I thought he was Nate's friend. I know 'stranger danger.' But I didn't consider him a stranger. His story made sense."

Megan had many questions about the how and why of Paul's involvement. Maybe he had slipped up and said something to Emma that would shed some light on the matter. "What did he tell you?"

"First, he said he was taking me somewhere safe while he and Nate looked for you. I kinda freaked out that you were missing. I was crying and everything." She picked at her pale-pink nail polish, her manicure ruined by the sea water. "He told me to stop being a baby, but I was so scared for you. Anyway, later that afternoon he made some phone calls and then he came back and said you had been found and were fine, but you needed to rest. I wanted to turn around and go straight home, but he made me feel really selfish for wanting to do that. After that he was really nice and he called the Owenses every night. They let me talk to him, even though we're not really allowed to have any phones or computers or anything during camp.

"I'm glad you cooperated." Megan stifled a shudder. She hoped Emma never realized what she and Nate had suffered—especially the mental anguish of what could have been happening to her. Much better to put this episode behind them with as little fanfare as possible.

"Yeah, and I'm really, really glad I got to go to dive camp," Emma said with an impish grin.

Megan couldn't help but laugh.

Emma leaned up against her in a sister cuddle. "Sooo, what's up with you and Nate?"

"Noth ... wha ... I don't know what you're talking about."

"Oh please, you're like Booth and Bones, Castle and Beckett—all 'we don't like each other' when everybody knows you're crazy attracted."

"Emma! When did you start watching crime shows?"

"I'm fourteen, practically an adult. Did you think I still watched Disney Channel?"

"Uh, yeah. Or at least Nickelodeon." Megan reached for her ringing phone. She listened for a few minutes, thanked the caller, and hung up. The lightheartedness fled the room.

Sobered, Emma asked, "What's going to happen to Nate?"

Megan tried to brighten her voice, but the words choked in her throat. "That was the attorney. He has a bail hearing set for tomorrow morning, so I guess we'll see what happens then."

"Can't we do something to help?"

Megan resumed rubbing Emma's back. "He thinks our testimony may help persuade the judge."

Emma looked up at her. "Yeah, we'll tell him Nate is innocent. He wouldn't hurt us." She snuggled back in.

"That's for the judge to decide. If he agrees, then maybe Nate can come home."

"We'd better pray for that judge."

"Yes, we'd better."

Inmates' curses and banging on the bars permeated the jail. There was a total lack of privacy, freedom, or control.

It's like being aboard ship.

But it wasn't. At sea, mental and physical training filled the days, followed by too few hours of rack time that passed in the blink of an eye. All too often, rescue dives interrupted sleep.

Here, the night stretched out unending before him. Sleep? Not a chance. His body was exhausted, but his mind raced. The answer seemed just out of reach, and the question eluded him.

The attorney Megan had called showed up. He was confident that the judge would approve bail, maybe even release Nate on his own recognizance. After all, Nate was a naval officer with a clean record. The evidence against him was circumstantial.

Circumstantial. That's all you ever had on Megan. Hope the judge isn't as hard as you.

"But we've cleared all that up. We're good now."

Are you? You still haven't asked her forgiveness. Still haven't apologized for your past treatment of her. You can't move forward until you've dealt with the past. You can't ignore it.

"Doesn't matter now. If I can't figure my way out of this mess..."

The Lord is trustworthy in all He promises; faithful in all He does.

"You've brought me this far, and although I don't understand any of this, I'm ready to trust that Your plan is better than mine. I'm handing off this mission to You."

Megan sat on the hard courtroom bench, hands folded, tension humming through her. Emma sat beside her spilling a constant stream of questions about their surroundings and the proceedings, none of which Megan could answer.

A fury of activity drew her eye to where Nate appeared in the doorway wearing a light-blue jumpsuit and handcuffs. He shuffled across the floor in leg shackles as a menacing armed guard escorted him to the defense table. As he stood at rigid attention, the judge read the charges against him.

Emma wrapped her hands around Megan's arm and inched closer to her.

"How do you plead?" The judge asked.

"Not guilty," Nate said with firm conviction.

The defense attorney Sonia had recommended spoke up. "Your Honor, we ask that the defendant be released on his own recognizance, but before you make that decision, the alleged victims are here and would like to make statements."

"You realize that will open the door to cross examination?"

"We welcome the prosecutor's input."

"Very well." The judge nodded. "Call your first witness."

Megan squeezed Emma's hand. "You'll do fine. Just tell the truth."

Emma shuffled to the stand. As the bailiff swore her in, her eyes darted back and forth between Megan and Nate.

The defense attorney approached her. "Hi Emma. Were you coerced into making a statement?"

"No."

"And did anyone tell you what to say?"

"No."

"Thank you. You may read your statement."

Emma unfolded the paper clutched in her hand and took a deep breath. "I'm glad that Nate is my big brother. He always spends lots of time with me when he's home and has taught me to do lots of cool things." Her thin voice strengthened as she gained confidence. "He would never hurt me, and I always feel really safe when I'm with him. I know he would never do anything bad, like the police say he did. That's just not Nate." When she finished she stood to leave.

"Wait just a minute." The prosecutor popped up. "Your Honor, if I may?"

"Proceed."

Emma remained standing and looked terrified. Megan shot her an encouraging smile. *C'mon on, you can do this brave girl.*

"Please sit, Ms. Harper. The accused is actually your half-brother, isn't that so?"

"Yes."

"And he's how much older than you?

Emma hesitated. "Twenty years."

"And before he so dramatically rescued you, when was the last time you had seen the defendant?"

"My birthday. He took me rock climbing."

"And your birthday was in...?"

"April."

"So you last saw him in April. You didn't spend time with him over the summer? Or Thanksgiving? Your dear brother wasn't present for this quintessential family holiday?"

"He ... he was deployed. He would have been there if he could." Emma sat on the edge of her seat and grabbed the railing that surrounded the witness box. "You have to believe me."

"Oh, I believe you, because up until a year ago holidays were the only time you saw him. He regularly requested duty stations that kept him far away from you. This brother who cares for you so deeply didn't make any effort to spend time with you."

"No, no, that's not true. He just didn't like..." Emma covered her mouth, the color draining from her face.

"What didn't he like?"

Megan held her breath. *How can this awful man know so much about us?*

"Ms. Harper, what didn't Nate like? Or should I be asking who?" Spreading his arms wide, he rested his hands on the railing in front of Emma and leaned in to block her view of the defense table. "Who kept your brother away from his family?"

The defense attorney broke in. "The prosecutor is badgering the witness. Your Honor, she's a child who has been through a horrific experience."

"Your Honor, if we release this girl's kidnapper, we would be putting her at greater risk than a few uncomfortable questions."

"We get your point, Counselor. The witness may step down."

Emma trembled as she made her way back to her seat. "I messed up really bad."

"No, honey, it's okay. It'll be fine." Megan patted her hand.

"Ms. Megan Foster, do you have a statement?" the defense attorney asked.

"Yes."

As Megan took her turn at the stand, she tried to catch Nate's eye, to assure him that everything was going to work out, but he sat erect with his military posture, eyes steady forward.

"Your statement, Ms. Foster?" The judge prompted.

"Yes, Your Honor." Willing her voice not to crack, Megan read her carefully-crafted letter. "I have known Nathan Harper for sixteen years. Although he comes from a wealthy family, he is not materialistic. In fact, in his chosen profession he helps people at great risk to his own life. He has a remarkable loyalty to his family and is especially kind and caring toward Emma. I simply cannot believe he would ever do anything that would harm her." As she folded the stationery, swallowing to irrigate her dry throat, the prosecutor rose.

"Yes, Mr. Prosecutor, you may question the witness. But keep it brief."

Megan tensed as the prosecutor approached. "Ms. Foster, when were you first aware that Emma was in danger?"

"Not until after ... when Nate found me in the alley."

"And if Mr. Harper is released, where will he go?"

She stared at Nate, willing him to look back. "I hope he'll come home." She turned to the judge. "He can leave the county, can't he? I mean, it's Christmas."

The judge nodded. "As long as he stays in the state. You would be comfortable with him around?"

"Of course. He belongs with family."

The prosecutor continued. "During this ... search, did Mr. Harper's behavior seem strange or different?"

Megan twisted her hands in her lap. "We were both under a lot of stress, but Nate was in control. He was smart and resourceful."

"Always one step ahead?"

She licked her lips. "No, we worked together."

"The charge is that he masterminded this kidnapping to force you to work with him on finding a secret formula."

"We were looking for a formula. That was the ransom demand. But Nate didn't mastermind it."

"Did your relationship change any?"

"Yes, we..." Heat rose up Megan's neck and she hesitated, unsure how to continue.

"Did he, maybe, manipulate your emotions?"

"No!"

But had he? Were those tender moments all a lie? She looked at Nate, begging him to confirm his feelings for her were real. But he sat, motionless as stone, never once glancing in her direction.

Chapter Seventeen

Every fiber in Nate's body wanted to jump up and yell, "Leave her alone." He pretended to stare ahead, but he could see the anguish in Megan's eyes, hear the torment in her voice.

He didn't know how she had done it, but she had managed to find an attorney willing to take his case—at least for the arraignment. And thanks be, the man seemed competent. Nate leaned over and whispered to him.

The attorney rose to his feet. "Your Honor, again, these questions are bordering on harassment. This witness came forward by her own volition. She's been under extreme pressure the last few days and was even kidnapped for a time herself. My client is innocent until proven guilty and his family, the victims, have made it clear they want him home for the holidays."

The prosecutor resumed his place at the other table. "Your Honor, precisely because the victims are family we recommend bail be denied. He already has undue influence over them and their testimonies."

A bailiff came down the aisle and whispered in the defense attorney's ear. The attorney looked down at Nate and then addressed the judge. "Your Honor, may I approach the bench?"

The two lawyers and the judge conferred in whispers for a few moments.

"Everybody to my chambers," the judge ordered.

"I think this is your lucky day," the attorney whispered as he led Nate down the hall to a conference room.

The judge sat at the head of the table with the two attorneys on either side. The court reporter set up her machine at the opposite end. Emma sat beside Nate and squeezed his hand under the table. He tried to give her a reassuring smile. Megan sat on the other side of Emma.

"Maybe they can clear this up," the judge grumbled. "Mr. Harper, you have an explanation for all of this?"

Nate blinked his eyes as George and Carol entered and sat across the table from him.

"I do, Your Honor." George Harper cleared his throat. "I've tried to instill strong principles, good character into my children. I always thought there was plenty of time, but a recent visit to my doctor made the matter more urgent. I still had lessons to teach them.

"So I created a puzzle that Nate and Megan would have to work together to solve. My purpose was two-fold. I knew if they combined their strengths, they would come to appreciate one another. Second, I've suffered many setbacks and disappointments in life, but the one thing that has always been constant is God's love for me and His forgiveness when I have miserably failed Him. I wanted them to learn to always place their trust in God above man."

Nate studied his folded hands. *This was a hard lesson, Dad.* Even though the situation had gone sideways, he was thankful for a father who made time for teachable moments.

"Where were you?" Megan asked. "The time we wasted trying to solve the puzzle could have been used to find Emma."

"I'm sorry about that, honey." Dark shadows rimmed his eyes, and for the first time Nate realized his father was aging. "I've been having some health issues. We didn't want to worry everyone this close to the holidays, and since we already had the vacation planned, we decided to utilize that time to have some tests done."

Nate shifted in his chair.

Megan echoed his thoughts. "Tests? Health problems?"

Carol spoke for the first time. "The good news is the tests came back negative, so it appears we have many years left to enjoy as a family."

George spread his hands on the table in an appeal to Nate and Megan. "The puzzle was meant for the two of you, and only at the time of my death. It never occurred to me that someone else would get wind of it." He turned back to the judge. "I don't know how Paul Spears learned about Devastation. But this isn't the first time someone has tried to steal one of our formulas. I doubt it will be the last. Corporate espionage is quite prevalent in the perfume industry."

Nate bowed his head.

"However, I am certain beyond a shadow of a doubt that Nate did not mastermind the kidnapping of Emma or manipulate Megan. I know my son. He is loyal and honorable. I'm sure everyone says such things about their children, but his reputation as a naval officer is spotless. So it's not just my word."

Nate's attorney looked at the judge. "In light of these facts, I make a motion that the charges against my client be dropped."

"You can file a motion, but I'll fight it," the prosecutor shot back.

All eyes turned to the judge, who stuffed papers into a folder and closed it. "I'm not ready to dismiss. Bring me the answer as to how Mr. Spears found out about Devastation or how those emails got on Mr. Harper's computer, and I'll be more inclined toward a dismissal. But for now, I will release Mr. Harper on his own recognizance." He looked at Nate. "You go home and enjoy Christmas with your family."

Nate brought the plane's engines to life as he contemplated the impossibility of the judge's words. How could he enjoy anything with a felony charge hanging over his head? His father, in the co-pilot's seat, read off the pre-flight checklist.

Behind him Emma chattered with Carol and Megan. Nate set the plane in motion down the runway. At least Emma and Megan were safe, even if he was in a legal tangle. Things could be much worse.

"Don't worry, son. My attorney will clean up this mess as soon as the holidays are over."

"Thanks Dad." He didn't voice his objection to having a corporate attorney work on his criminal case. His dad meant well, just like he meant well when he created the puzzle. It had worked in a sense. He had gotten to really know Megan instead of making surface judgments. And by knowing her, he'd come to care for her. Not merely the physical attraction he had fought over the years but a deep, emotional bond forged through the adversity they had faced together.

Too bad you blew it.

Even though it was over for him, he was determined to find out who was behind this scheme. He couldn't believe that Spears would do this on his own, un-coerced. Or maybe his pride refused to admit he could make such a bad character judgment.

The return trip passed without incident, and they were soon debarking at the air field in Jacksonville. Megan grasped his hand as he assisted her down the plane steps. She squeezed it and held on, even after she reached the ground. She didn't let go until he assisted her into the backseat of the Hummer. His father had taken the front passenger seat, and Nate reminded himself it was only natural for him to do so as the head of the family.

As Carol ushered Emma into the seat next to Megan, Nate figured they couldn't know about the change that had taken place in his and Megan's relationship. They had always been awkward, unable to get through a conversation without a personality clash, so they had avoided one another whenever the family was together.

Although, he thought Carol might suspect something. She had given him a strange look a few times. Of course, that could be because her step-son was about to be a convicted felon and her daughter was the victim. Except, he had to admit Carol had been very kind today. She had hugged him when they left the judge's chambers and told him she was praying for him. And for the first time he was kind back—not forced politeness, but sincere appreciation. She had supported his dad through a health scare and it was evident that they did love one another. He glanced in the rear view mirror and caught Megan's eye. He wanted her beside him so he could hold her hand and admit that she had breached his defenses—admit that he loved her.

Then reality crashed in on him. He broke eye contact and surveyed the road ahead. He couldn't saddle her with his feelings. Things sounded pretty positive in the judge's chambers this morning, but what if the motions failed? What if the judge decided not to dismiss the charges? The prosecutor was adamant that he wasn't dropping the charges. A long trial, possible felony conviction and prison. He couldn't put Megan through that. She didn't owe him any loyalty and he wouldn't ask for it.

He pulled under the portico, and everyone piled out of the vehicle.

"I know we're all tired," Carol said. "Let's rest awhile. We'll leave for dinner at eight."

Nate walked around to the back of the Hummer. "Dad, let me help you with the luggage, then I'll head home. Wash the jail stink off me."

Carol hesitated at the door. "Just put it in the laundry room. I'll deal with it later. Much later."

Once the luggage was unloaded, Nate said his goodbyes.

George patted him on the back. "I couldn't be prouder of you, son. God is in control. He'll work this out."

"Thanks." He stuck out his hand, and George grabbed it and pulled him into a hug.

Carol touched his arm. "You're in my prayers every day."

Nate pulled free of his dad's arms and turned to his step-mom. "Carol, I owe you an apology. I've been cold and judgmental toward you when you've shown me nothing but kindness. I had no right to condemn your marriage to Dad. The two of you make a good match. I realized that today. You stood by me when I haven't proven my innocence, but you still believe in me." He stopped, not sure what to do when he saw the tears streaming down her face. She settled the question, drawing him into a hug. Years of resentment washed away as he hugged her back.

"You don't know how much that means to me." Carol dabbed her eyes.

A weight rolled off Nate's shoulders. Holding back—throwing up walls—had been exhausting. He was relieved to end the silent war with Carol. And for the first time since his mother died, he felt part of a family.

Emma came running down the stairs. "I was afraid I missed you!"

He chuckled. "I'll be back in a few hours for dinner."

"Really? You're really coming with us? To church too?"

"I'm really coming with you." He pinched her nose.

She swatted at him. "Stop that." But her laughter took out the sting.

He looked around for Megan. He owed her an explanation for his change of attitude, and he needed to release her from any obligation she might feel. He found her leaning against the breakfast bar and smiling at the happy banter.

"Walk you home?" He ignored the family's raised eyebrows and knowing smiles.

Megan accepted Nate's outstretched hand, longing for some precious alone time with him. He had been so cold and distant since his arrest. Of course, he had a lot on his plate, but she wished he would turn to her for comfort. She believed in him and his innocence. After all, she loved him.

They crossed the lawn in silence. She wanted him to be the first to speak. Wanted to know what he was thinking so she could address his concerns, put him at ease. A biting wind blew off the ocean and she shivered. She moved in close to his side and pulled the hand she held around her shoulder, expecting him to laugh and squeeze her closer.

Instead, he released her hand, tugged off his jacket, and placed it on her shoulders. At the door, he took the key from her and unlocked it. Then he swung it open and gestured for her to enter.

She stepped across the threshold, turned, and invited him in, but he remained on the porch. "Nate?"

He scrubbed a hand over his face and refused to make eye contact. "This isn't fair to you Megan."

"This whole thing is unfair. How could anyone think that—"

"That I took advantage of you? That I manipulated you?" He turned to leave, then stopped with his back to her. "You have doubts. Go ahead, admit it. Deep down you're wondering."

"No." She shook her head.

He strode toward her. "The prosecution is going to call you to testify."

"You think this is about intimidating or influencing a witness?" Megan moved a step closer. "It's never going to get to that point. You're innocent." She clasped his face in her hands, forcing him to look her in the eye. Then, standing on tiptoes, she drew him close and brushed her lips against his.

His arms pulled her into a tight embrace as he lifted her off the ground and deepened the kiss. His lips left hers, and he fluttered kisses across her cheeks.

She hummed as his light touch cheered her. Squelching his ridiculous worries, she rested her head against his shoulder. "We'll beat this together, Nate."

His arms tightened around her until she thought she would stop breathing. Moments later he lowered her feet to the ground. "No, I have to fight this battle alone." He took a step back, tightening fists by his sides.

"I'll stand by you." She tried to pull him back into her embrace, but he remained rooted in place.

"No," he caressed her cheek, "you need to forget about me."

"But Nate, I lo—"

"Shhh…" He placed a finger to her lips.

She studied his eyes, and then, jaw set, he turned and trudged across the lawn.

Megan pulled his jacket closer around her and breathed in his scent. She couldn't understand why he wouldn't let her in. Hadn't she proven herself to him yet? Didn't he see he could trust her? In the distance, the Hummer's engine came to life, followed by the squeal of tires.

As she turned to head back into the cottage, she heard a rustling. She craned her neck and squinted, peering into the darkness to see if anyone was around. After the last few days, she wasn't past paranoia. When she determined it was nothing, she pushed open the unlocked door and drifted into the cottage.

She wasn't the same girl she was a week ago. She had risen to every challenge thrown at her and had won, and she wasn't about to give up now. She had found her inner strength, and she was going to fight. She wouldn't lose Nate. Not to injustice. And not to Paul's deceit.

Nate drove the coastal road to the ferry that would take him home. He couldn't forget the sweetness of Megan's lips or the hurt in her eyes when he rejected her.

You're a fool, Nate Harper, a fool to let pride ruin your life.

"If I can clear my name, prove beyond a shadow of a doubt that I had anything to do with the kidnapping..."

The French connection file from Spears's computer stuck in his brain. Someone was behind this, masterminding the whole thing, and with a name like Benoit...

Nate spun the steering wheel hard left, turned the Hummer 180 degrees, and floored the gas.

He'd be willing to bet the Amelia Island Police Department had never heard of Silva and Benoit. After all, they'd shown up at the most inopportune times. How could they have known where he and Megan would be, unless they were watching or setting them up?

Nate was surprised when the officer at the front desk of AIPD not only knew Silva and Benoit but sent him back to their desks with an escort.

Nate stood in awkward silence before the two detectives. He had been so sure they were fakes he didn't know what to say after learning they were authentic.

"Sit." Benoit indicated a chair beside the desk. He opened a drawer and pulled out a laminated card. "Here's Emma's ID. Glad to hear she was found safe."

"Hey man, I'm sorry I gave you such a hard time about Megan's bruises." Silva slapped Nate on the shoulder. "But you were acting kind of suspicious."

"Yeah, about that..."

Benoit dismissed his explanation with a wave of his hand. "If you were involved, you'd have come up with a better story. We understand the pressure of the constraints you were under."

Nate took the chair Benoit offered. "Why did you keep showing up?"

"We kept getting anonymous tips letting us know when Paul Spears was supposed to be making drug buys," Benoit said. "We'd been trying to catch a local drug dealer for several months without success, so following a potential buyer was a good lead for us."

"Did you ever track down the source?"

"No, and we never caught him making a buy. But he was using. We searched his apartment and found plenty of evidence." Benoit leaned back in his chair. "Our investigation found he was up to his eyeballs in debt. The pills didn't seem to be affecting his work performance, but he had lost several clients recently. Word was getting around that he was addicted and unreliable, but no one we talked to had specific examples to back that up. All the clients we talked to were pleased with his work. Even the ones who had dropped him. They were just being cautious."

"This all started in the last four or five months. Before that, his business was rock solid," Silva said.

"And, even though we were tipped on times and places, we never saw him buying any drugs," Benoit added.

Puzzled, Nate looked back and forth between the two men. "But the Key West Police said you had surveillance tapes."

Silva crossed his ankles on the desk. "Yeah. They were mailed to us. We didn't take them."

"So somebody was setting him up for a scheme like this."

"And boy, was he nervous," Benoit said. "He almost had a heart attack every time we showed up."

Nate didn't like this one bit. It was clear that Spears had a partner who was still at large. It couldn't be Otto. He had escaped the police in Key West, but he was all brawn, no brain. Whoever had masterminded this plan was clever.

"What about Miles Bentley?" Nate asked.

The detectives looked at each other. "Who?" Silva asked.

Nate shook his head. "Never mind." Bentley was probably another pawn in their game. Then, he remembered what had brought him here in the first place.

"So Benoit, I guess you're not the French Connection, huh?"

"I'm about as French as a French fry." Benoit chuckled. "What's the French Connection?"

Nate rose to his feet. "I think it's the answer to who's behind all this."

"Do you have any idea who that might be?" Silva asked.

Nate shook his head. "No. But then, I was never involved with the business, which is why this doesn't make sense. I didn't know anything about Devastation. How did Spears find out about it?"

"That's a good question. We'll be sure to ask him about that."

"Spears is here?"

"Yep, Key West sent him back north. The Jacksonville Sheriff's Office is way backlogged on their caseload, so we won the jurisdiction battle. He arrived about fifteen minutes ago."

"We're about to interrogate him, see if he'll spill the beans on his partner. Wanna watch?"

"Sure."

They stood, and Nate followed the detectives down the hall.

Silva opened the door to the observation room and waited for Nate to enter. "You can see and hear everything through the two-way mirror, but he can't see or hear you. If you need to communicate with us, tell the tech." He nodded to a woman sitting at a desk and manning several computer consoles.

"Thanks," Nate said, hoping the glass would help him contain his anger when he saw Spears again.

What he observed was a broken man. The cocky, self-assured Paul looked haggard and resigned. Something Nate never expected of him. But then again, he never expected his betrayal either. Nate tried to be angry, tried to wish the worst for Paul, but he found he couldn't. He had sat innocent in the judgment seat, and now he found it difficult to judge someone else's actions without hearing the whole story. The accident, painkillers, some rumors, and now his life spiraled out of control. Why hadn't he seen his friend's desperation?

Nate watched as Silva and Benoit entered the room. Benoit sat in front of Paul, while Silva paced behind him. Not being able to see that guy would drive Nate nuts. Of course, that was their plan.

He wondered how it felt for Spears to be under the very interrogation techniques he'd employed throughout his career. Did it give him an advantage, or did he know his goose was cooked? Would he call for his attorney and refuse to answer any questions or make a deal—betray a partner for his freedom? Nate counted on betrayal.

Benoit opened the file and studied it, giving Spears time to get good and nervous. "Devastation."

Spears stared at him, never blinking an eye.

"We've got you on drug possession and kidnapping. But we know you didn't do this alone. All we care about is your partner. Give us a name and these other charges..."

Spears leaned forward, folding his hands on the table. "I could lawyer up and take my chances in court."

"You could. But you won't. Deep down you care about this family, and you're going to do the right thing."

Spears studied his hands.

"Nate says you're a man of integrity. He's willing to hear your side of the story, even after you betrayed him. Your muddy mess splattered all over him. Don't you owe him some kind of explanation?"

Spears looked at the glass.

Nate backed up a step, certain Paul could see right through to him. It was unnerving.

"Is Harper out there? Nate, I swear man, the drugs, the money problems—it was all a set up. She framed me the same as she did you. The only thing I'm guilty of is falling for the wrong woman." Paul slumped down in his chair.

"What's her name?" Benoit prodded.

"He had the good sense to steer clear of her." Paul pointed his chin toward the glass. "Of course, he had Megan. Only a fool would jeopardize that."

Nate shifted in discomfort at the truth. He was a fool to take so long to admit his love for Megan. He hadn't hidden his feelings as well as he thought. But what did that have to do with this other woman? Nate searched his brain for someone Paul had met through him who was connected to Megan.

Spears was still talking. "She was good, had me spilling my guts about the accident. In no time she realized I was still taking narcotic painkillers. Although I had legal prescriptions, it was easy enough for her to plant some street drugs in my apartment. That's when she had me. From there, she kept building a frame. She knew so much about me. In my line of work, I should have known better, but she was hypnotic. I gave her access to every part of my life. When I realized what she was up to, it was too late."

Silva leaned over his shoulder. "So you chose to betray your friend and his family—a child—for this woman?"

"I could have gotten out of her frame, maybe, but I knew she'd never give up on Devastation. I could have turned her and her plot over to Nate or the police, but there was no evidence whatsoever to back up my story, and my character was shot—she had made sure of that." Spears sat up in his chair and spoke with more conviction. "It was better for me to be her patsy. At least then I could keep an eye on the situation, steer Nate in the right direction, and keep Emma safe. I made it a condition of my cooperation that I took care of Emma during and after the kidnapping. Of course, if she had wanted to, she could have refused. I had no leverage. But it served her purpose, kept her removed from the crime and from getting her hands dirty. And it gave me the opportunity to make sure that Emma came through this with as little trauma and scarring as possible."

"Convinced yourself your actions were justified, huh?" Silva slammed the table in front of Spears.

"That should count for something Nate, don't you think?" Spears's gaze pierced through the glass.

Why didn't you speak up sooner? Nate still wasn't sure Paul was being sincere.

As if he heard his silent question, Spears continued. "Otto was there watching my every move. And I didn't know about the emails she placed in Nate's account until later. When the police showed up at the dive camp, I thought it was over—Nate and Megan would get Emma back, I'd do time for my stupidity."

"Yet you still refused to give the name of your partner."

"Once I realized what she had done to Nate, I knew it was going to take more time to unravel this web. I needed some time to think and strategize. It's not easy staying ahead of that minx."

Forgetting protocol, Nate banged on the window. "I know who it is!"

Megan woke with a start. A noise? Probably just the wind. She peeked out the window where all was ghostly quiet. A creaking sound spun her around. She listened for a moment then relaxed. The pipes in the old cottage often creaked as the water warmed in the heater.

She yawned as she looked at the clock. Time for a long, hot bath before dinner. She padded into the bathroom and sat on the edge of the tub, letting the water splash over her hand. God had been so good. They had found Emma unscathed, and the whole family was home again. They would have a wonderful dinner tonight and spend Christmas Day together tomorrow. This could be the perfect Christmas, except once again she and Nate were at odds.

Of course he was worried about the charges against him, and she was too. But she was confident they would be dismissed. They were ridiculous. Anyone could see how much he loved Emma.

But his words haunted her. He didn't need to manipulate her. She was helping anyway.

He knew you'd do anything for Emma.

That didn't mean he arranged to have Emma kidnapped. She pushed the thought away.

A loud thud caught her attention, and she turned off the faucet to listen better. It came from the living room. Not really a knocking sound, more of a banging. She went to investigate. As she rounded the corner, the door frame splintered and 300-pound Otto surged into her home.

Ice ran through Megan's veins and instinct took over. She ran for the back door, overturning a kitchen chair behind her. It crashed to the floor as Otto lunged for her. She reached for the knob, fumbling to unlock the deadbolt with her other hand.

Otto tossed the chair out of his way, his face purple with rage.

Her fingers refused to work right as she pulled and pushed on the door while turning the handle. When it finally swung open, it did so with such force she almost lost her footing. Relief flooded through her as she came face to face with her friend.

"Sonia! We've got to get outta here." Megan tried to push Sonia out the door, but she stood firm.

Otto grabbed Megan from behind, lifting her up in the air with her arms pinned at her sides. She screamed and kicked with all her might, landing a few blows that only served to make Otto squeeze her tighter.

Sonia walked past them into the kitchen and righted the chair. "*Halten sie nieder.* Hold her down while I tie the ropes."

"Sonia? What are you doing? You can't be behind this. You're our attorney, my friend."

Otto slammed her into the chair and held her down by the shoulders while Sonia secured each ankle to a chair leg with practiced efficiency.

"Oh, spare me the anguish. Our so-called friendship was carefully cultivated. I knew sooner or later I would find the information I needed, but I had to have the trust of someone high up in the company, preferably a family member. You fit the bill perfectly."

Sonia passed the rope to Otto, and he tied Megan's arms behind the chair back. "We will play a little game of truth or dare. I dare you not to tell me the truth. Where is the real formula for Devastation?" Gone were her colloquial Americanisms, now she spoke in the same stilted manner as Otto.

"I've told you, Devastation doesn't exist."

Sonia slapped her hard across the face. "Liar. I've waited for years for this opportunity. So I make friends with you and then I visit you in the lab for lunch. I go through your files when you step out of the office for a moment. And I get little tidbits. Nothing."

Reeling from the blow, Megan fought to convince Sonia of the facts. "It was a team-building exercise George created to help me and Nate learn to work together."

Sonia appeared back in front of her. "I knew George's plan. I drew up the will."

"The ingredients made up a puzzle. It wasn't about perfume. It was about life." Megan twisted against the ropes. "Why are you doing this?"

"My ancestors were perfumers in Russia for centuries, until it was all taken away from us and our family exiled to Germany. Now we have a chance to rebuild our fortune, but the recipes have all been lost, destroyed by cretins. My brother Ivan went to France. He was so close to success, but as he was leaving the laboratory the police cornered him and shot him. He had set off a silent alarm system so he was killed—no, murdered—for trying to regain what was stolen from us."

"What's that got to do with Harper Scents?"

"You gave an excellent talk at the International Perfumers Convention in Grasse, France two years ago, no? Synthesizing natural elements? You could make any scent from a few chemicals. That is what we needed. So I am sent to the States on a mission, our last hope." Sonia paced around the chair, waving her arms for emphasis. "My mother's family is calling me. 'Sonia, when will you have the formulas? We need the formulas. We're all counting on you.' They put so much pressure on me I think of killing myself. I promise them no member of the Harper family will be safe until I have all the formulas." She leaned down into Megan's face. "The judge hasn't dismissed the charges against Nate yet. I can make the frame I built air tight. He'll be convicted of Emma's kidnapping, your murder and spend his life in prison."

Megan didn't flinch. Looking Sonia in the eyes, she said, "You can have all the formulas. I don't care."

Sonia straightened up and turned. "Good. But we must have Devastation, or no deal."

"There is no..."

Sonia whirled around. "Stupid woman. I will take you to Russia with me. We could use a chemist with your talents." She motioned to the large man. "Stay, Otto. Keep her quiet, but no marks. It will make it harder to get her through customs."

Sonia disappeared, but Megan heard her opening and slamming drawers in the bedroom. "You must have a passport."

Megan tried to ignore Otto, who stood, arms crossed, a menacing stare fixed on her.

"If I failed, my family would disown me. I would be nothing, have nothing." Sonia's voice carried from the bedroom. "Then you invited me to the Fourth of July party, and I met Nate. Now, I think. I can make a man do anything for me. But he is only interested in you, and you do not even know it." She cackled. "He brought his stupid friend for you, and you do not even see him. So Paul and I wind up in a corner, discussing our mutual problem, and I see the solution."

Can I outrun Otto? Megan measured the distance to the door. First, she had to get loose.

"Ah, I found your passport." Sonia entered the kitchen holding up the blue book in triumph. She slipped it into her coat pocket.

"Immediately I knew he was weak, that I could manipulate him. I had only to find his price. Then I realized he was hooked on pain pills. I spread some rumors ... he is a drug addict." Sonia paced in front of Megan. "Someone died because he was high and did not protect them. Soon he was losing clients, and that led to money problems. Now I only had to wait for George to leave town, the company to shut down for the holidays. Your father ... such a generous man."

"He is generous. I'm sure he would help you reestablish your family's business in Russia. He could give you a loan, maybe some equipment..."

"Yes, I'll take a loan." She stopped in front of Megan, leaned over, and pointed at her. "You. Otto, you have the *drogen*, the ketamine?"

Chapter Eighteen

Nate jogged up to the cottage porch. Mere hours ago he had held Megan in his arms, enjoying the sweetness of her kiss. Praying he wasn't too late, he berated himself for leaving her alone, for not seeing a deeper plot.

He reached for the door handle and froze. The doorframe was cracked, preventing the door from closing. Nate backed away and, bending over, skirted around the cottage to the back door. Peeking in through the kitchen window, he saw the hefty wrestler type from the alley and the Jet Ski. Otto, Paul had called him, stood leaning against the kitchen door with his arms crossed. He stared at Megan, who was tied to a chair.

Pulse pounding, Nate prepared to burst through the door when a tall, dark-haired woman entered from the living room pulling a suitcase behind her.

Nate jerked back from the window, flattening himself against the wall. His instincts were dead on, thanks to Paul's clue. He leaned in for another quick look and saw the waves of jet-black hair flowing down her back.

His suspicions were confirmed. *Sonia.* The friend Megan had tried to set him up with at the Fourth of July picnic. Her exotic, dark beauty would have tempted him if he weren't already in love with a petite blonde.

Admit it Harper. You've got it bad.

"It won't matter if I blow this," he muttered under his breath.

Ducking under the window, he used his cell phone to send a text. He prayed it was received in time.

Another glance through the window verified Otto's and Sonia's positions. He tossed a couple of pebbles at the window and waited in the darkness. When Otto came out to investigate, Nate snuck up from behind and kicked him in the back of the knees. As he went down, Nate grabbed him around the neck and neutralized him. Then he dragged him into the bushes.

"Otto? What's going on out there?" Sonia stood in the kitchen doorway.

Nate wasn't in position to nab Sonia, so he waited for his prey to come to him.

Sonia turned and went back into the kitchen. "Time's up, Foster. Looks like you're taking an extended vacation."

Nate crept around the hedge to the back door and peered in.

Sonia rummaged through a duffle bag until she pulled something out. Holding up the syringe, she uncapped the needle and approached Megan.

"No!"

Sonia turned toward the voice, eyes wide as Nate came at her in a flying tackle. His arms stretched out to wrap around her legs, but when he landed on the floor, his arms were empty. He started to scramble to his feet, her words stopping him cold.

"Don't move."

She stood behind Megan, the needle held against her neck.

Nate remained in a crouched position. "Okay, I'm not going anywhere." He raised his hands in submission.

"Otto!" Sonia called out, keeping her eyes locked on Nate. Her call met silence. "*Bruder*, get in here!"

Nate measured the distance between him and Megan. Could he reach her before Sonia plunged the needle? He sized up Sonia. She was getting nervous that her brother wasn't responding, but would she incapacitate Megan before she went looking for him? He caught Megan's eye and saw a gleam there. She had a plan. He blinked his eyes in acknowledgement and waited for her to make her move.

When Megan toppled the chair over, Sonia's eyes widened, then she took off running.

Nate lunged forward to catch her as she tried to escape out the front door. She tried to stick him with the needle, but he caught her wrist, bending it until, with a grunt, she released it. Turning her over, he brought her arms together behind her back. He looked around for something to secure her and heard footsteps coming through the front door.

"Looks like you've done all the heavy lifting," Benoit said.

"Yeah, but I could use some cuffs."

"Sure, we'll take it from here." Benoit slapped a pair of handcuffs on Sonia.

Nate rushed back to Megan. "Good move." He lifted her and the chair into an upright position. Kneeling in front of her, he worked with nimble fingers to untie her hands and feet.

Once she was free, he smoothed the hair off her cheek and paused a moment to drink in her beauty. He took her face into his hands and drew her close, kissing her with a slow, lingering kiss.

"Hey Lover Boy, if you wanna get these clowns processed, we're going to need statements from the two of you."

Nate pulled back, clearing his throat. "Yeah, I want to get this over with. I've got plans to make."

Megan leaned over the kitchen sink and splashed cold water on her face. Through the window, she watched as Silva pulled a half-conscious Otto out of the bushes.

She turned away with a shudder and wandered into the living room. Sonia sat stony-faced and handcuffed on the couch while Benoit sifted through the suitcase.

"Are these your things?"

She glanced at the familiar clothing and nodded, unable to form words.

He zipped the suitcase closed and stood, positioning himself between her and Sonia. "We don't need these things, so you can take them to your room." He handed over her passport and luggage.

She moved down the hallway, numb to her surroundings. How could Sonia have done such a horrible thing? The thought made her sick and she rushed to the bathroom. When she came out, Nate and Benoit were conversing in hushed tones.

"...ticket for Megan Foster."

"To Russia? Oh, no, we would have never..." Nate shot her a quizzical look and broke off his words.

Benoit placed a hand on her shoulder. "We're taking Otto and Sonia to the station for booking. You and Nate can follow us. I promise it won't take long and then you can meet up with your family. I understand you're having dinner together?"

"Um, I don't..." Her appetite had fled, but having family around sounded comforting. "Yes, yes. That's right."

"Okay, I'm leaving you in Nate's care."

Nate opened his arms and she slumped into them.

"Let's get this scum out of here," Silva said to Benoit as he wrestled Otto through the door.

"Right behind ya." Benoit hoisted Sonia from the couch and proceeded out, struggling to close the broken door behind him.

Tension fled as silence filled the cottage, now empty except for Megan and Nate.

"I'll rig that door so you're safe tonight, unless you want to sleep in the main house? There are plenty of rooms." Nate rubbed her back as she circled her arms around his waist and snuggled in closer to him.

"Mmm."

"You're exhausted. I'll call Benoit and postpone until later."

"No, tomorrow's Christmas, so I'd rather get this done and over with tonight." She pulled herself up straight. "Why did you come back?"

"I'll tell you all about it on the way." He wrapped his arm around her shoulder and led her to the Hummer.

Megan sat in the interview room of the Amelia Island Police Department, sipping on the cup of water they'd allowed her. Nate was in a separate room, giving his version of the night's events. It was déjà vu all over again. The scenario had not ended well in Key West—what would be the outcome tonight? She couldn't get over the shock that Sonia, her best friend, who she shared everything with, had betrayed her. All this time, Sonia had been using their friendship to feed her own greed. Megan understood how Nate must have felt when he found out Paul had been behind Emma's kidnapping.

Detective Silva entered the room and sat across the table. "We just have a few things to clear up." He opened a folder and slid a picture over to her. "Do you recognize this man?"

Megan's stomach heaved as she stared down at the image of Miles Bentley beaten, bruised, and quite dead. She buried her head in her hands. *Will this nightmare ever end?*

"He was found in the Harper Scents laboratory with this paper." He pulled out the yellow sheet Nate had torn from the legal pad the night they made the mad dash to the nativity scene. "It appears he was mixing the ingredients from this list." He moved around the table and crouched beside her. "Look, we're not accusing you of anything. We just need all the facts."

"Miles Bentley, he was a chemist, one of our researchers. They probably wanted him to test the formula." Megan combed a hand through her hair. "He offered to help me, but I don't know ... someone was shooting at us ..."

"That fits what we've pieced together. Interpol says he's one of theirs, here to investigate a murder in France tied to a perfume manufacturer."

"Sonia's brother, Ivan, was killed by police in France."

"Yeah, well, not before he murdered the owner's son and shot down two officers."

Shuddering, Megan whispered, "It's just perfume."

"Not to these people." Silva laid a notepad in front of her. "Write down everything you can remember. No rush."

While reviewing the events of the evening, she tried to think of anything she could have done that would have saved Miles Bentley.

Silva returned with a cup of coffee.

"I keep running it through my mind. I should have known he was a cop, or I should have trusted him or done something different..."

Silva placed the coffee in front of her. "It's not your fault. He was working undercover, so he couldn't tell you who he was. Besides, the coroner places his time of death around four a.m. This all went down long after you were gone."

"But if I..." She breathed in the coffee's rich aroma and released it in a sigh.

"I know it's hard, but you have to put this behind you. If he, a professional, couldn't stop this, then there's no way you could have." He patted her hand. "Nate told me how courageous you've been through this ordeal. Don't underestimate your role in saving Emma. Hold onto that."

She tipped her head to the side and looked at him, eyes wide. "You know Nate had nothing to do with this?"

"Yeah, we know. The charges against him have been dropped."

An hour later, Megan walked out of the interview room with mixed emotions. She was elated to be free but saddened by Miles Bentley's death and hurt by Sonia's betrayal.

Carol and Emma greeted her in the hallway with hugs and tears of joy.

"I know this has been horrible for you, but we have so much to be thankful for. George's health, our family's safety." Carol kissed Megan's cheek. "We'll make Christmas memories that will wipe out all the bad ones."

"Nate and Daddy will meet us at the restaurant," Emma said.

"I think George has invited the whole town." Carol wrapped her arm around Megan's shoulder and pulled her close as they headed for the door.

Megan welcomed their comfort, but she longed for someone else's embrace. She glanced over Emma's head to where George was congratulating Nate. She thought she caught his eye, but Benoit came out and blocked her view. She would have to wait.

Emma chattered while Carol drove them to the restaurant. The men followed in the Hummer. Silva and Benoit were off-duty for the night and would arrive soon with their families for the impromptu celebration.

Throughout dinner, Megan cast surreptitious glances at Nate, trying to gage his mood or reactions to the night's events. The intimate family dinner for five had doubled, and Nate sat so far down the table, conversation was impossible. On the few occasions that she managed to catch his eye, any meaningful exchange was interrupted by the continual stream of family friends and business acquaintances stopping by to wish them a Merry Christmas.

By the time dinner ended, the group joining them on the stroll to the church had quadrupled. Megan walked along side Mrs. Cratz, an elderly woman whose hilarious stories were legendary, though somewhat exaggerated.

At the church, they sang Christmas carols. The nativity scene players performed the story of Jesus' birth, and then the congregation lit candles while singing "Silent Night." The pastor prayed for peace on earth and goodwill toward men in the coming year.

Some people moved out of the pews to the front of the church to offer personal thanksgiving. Nate was in prayer at the altar when the congregants reverently filed out of the sanctuary with their lighted candles.

Swept along with the family back to the estate, Megan heard the church bells chime midnight. Another day gone, and she still didn't know where she stood with Nate.

Early the next morning, Megan strung popcorn as she watched Emma decorate the tree, but her mind was a million miles away. Well, not a million. Just across the intra-coastal to a particular house in Mayport. What was Nate doing right now? And what did he mean last night when he said he had plans to make? It didn't seem those plans would include her.

"Megan, Meeegan where are you?"

It took a moment for Emma's sing-song voice to break through her thoughts. "I'm sorry, what were you saying?"

"We need more popcorn."

Nate shifted the duffle bag filled with gifts from one hand to the other while he waited for Megan to answer his knock. This mission was like none other he had ever attempted. He had no experience and was going in untrained and unarmed. He had checked his armor at the front walkway and was willing to take whatever pain she dished out.

The prayer he began at the altar last night had continued until this morning. He had a choice to make. He could allow Paul's betrayal to fortify his wall and continue to exist in solitude, or he could embrace the love and forgiveness Christ had shown him and live a full and happy life.

I came so you could have an abundant life. Why would you refuse that?

"Why indeed?" he whispered. At last, he had peace and clarity about the direction of his life and his relationship with Megan. No more ignoring the emotional upheavals of his life. He was ready to share and help others on their journey through difficulties. After all, he was a trainer. And he had seen plenty of men who needed this type of training—himself included. Time enough for that later, though. Right now he was facing the fight of his life, one he wouldn't quit until he had won—the battle for Megan's heart.

But when the door opened he could only stare at her. All the practiced lines left his mind as he soaked in her natural beauty.

"Nate, what are you doing here?" Megan said as she stepped out onto the porch and pulled the door closed behind her. She shivered as the cold ocean breeze whipped around the corner of the cottage.

He dropped the duffle bag and shrugged out of his jacket, placing it around her thin shoulders. Resting his hands there, he cleared his throat. "I was wrong. I let pride and stupidity cloud my judgment, but if you can find a way to forgive me, I will make it my mission..." She tried to break in, but he stopped her. "I'm not worthy. I know that. I'm just asking for a chance to prove..."

Megan placed a finger on his lips. "I forgave you a long time ago. And your worth doesn't need proving. Not to me."

Nate was afraid to move—afraid he would wake up from this dream. But he could taste salt on her finger and smell popcorn in the air, so was he dreaming? Could she really want him?

Emma opened the door and broke the spell. "You're under the mistletoe. Kiss her."

Nate didn't check the veracity of her statement. Instead, he sought permission from Megan.

She framed his face in her hands and pulled him toward her.

He bent down and with feather-lightness brushed her lips with his.

She returned the favor.

Wrapping his arms around her waist, he lifted her off the ground and deepened the kiss, lost in the flavor of her.

"Yay!" Emma clapped her hands together.

Embarrassed, Nate drew back and set Megan on the ground.

Megan laughed but tightened her arms around his neck and tilted his head down for another lingering taste.

Aware of Emma watching, Nate broke away from Megan's salty sweetness with reluctance.

Emma emitted another giggle, and he gave her a stern look from over Megan's head. "You, young lady, have a lot to learn about privacy."

When Emma looked with uncertainty from one to the other, Nate held out his arm and pulled her into a side hug. "Good call, kiddo."

Megan wrapped her arm around Emma and latched onto Nate's elbow. "Group hug!"

Nate squeezed both girls, then turned back to Megan, tightening his grip on her waist. "I love you, Megan Foster."

Her eyes lit up like the glow of the Christmas tree inside the front window. "Finally. I had given up hope of ever winning your heart."

"You've had it from the day I first saw you. I just didn't know how to say it."

"Then let me show you. I love you, Nate Harper." As their lips met again, she left no room for doubt.

Dear Reader,

I hope you enjoyed reading the story of Nate and Megan as much as I did writing it.

The idea for the romance in My Sister's Keeper came from my own family history. In the early 1940s my grandmother became a widow and a single mother. Eventually she married an older man with a grown son in the Navy. On a visit home, the son realized that the awkward tomboy step-sister he had previously ignored had blossomed into a beautiful young woman. Thus began a lifelong marriage.

Several couples have shared similar experiences with me. In these stories, the family dynamics are especially intriguing when they involve half-siblings who are significantly younger. I love this back story for my characters, Nate and Megan. Despite their animosity toward each other, they both dearly love their half-sister, fourteen-year-old Emma.

As Megan learned, finding our hero isn't always easy, even when he's right in front of us. With patience, prayer, and a little stretching outside her comfort zone, she became the heroine Nate needed to rescue him from his emotional prison.

If you liked this story, please tell your friends and take a moment to leave a review for this book at your favorite retailer.

Now, go be a heroine!

Dalyn

About Dalyn Woods

As a fan of crime dramas, Dalyn enjoys writing characters who dance that beautiful waltz of romance. For added dimension, she weaves faith and suspense into the music.

My Sister's Keeper is her debut novel with two more in the works. Exposed and the The Bride Escape are coming fall of 2020. She is also blogging a nonfiction book on relationships, Finding Your Hero, Being His.

A lifelong resident of Northeast Florida, she enjoys big city convenience, beaches along the Atlantic Coast, and the wild beauty of Old Florida.

A little piece of wilderness is preserved on the three-acre homestead she shares with her husband of more than 25 years and cats of varying number, but always one short of being a 'crazy cat lady'.

Printed in Great Britain
by Amazon

54574407R00152